WHY THE CAPTAIN DID NOT MARRY

a play by

Guðbjörg Elinborg Þórðardóttir

edited by Iris E Ferrier and James McD Ferrier

ISBN: 9798387546174
Imprint: Independently published

EDITOR'S PREFACE

Why the Captain did not Marry was written by Gudbjorg Elinborg Thordardottir (also known as Ella Thordar). A copy of the type-written script was rediscovered amongst her papers in January 2023. We do not know the exact year of writing, but it is understood that the script, prepared in English, was written after Elinborg attended a Pitman typing course in England in 1928. It has been a great privilege to undertake the editing of the play and to gain an insight into Elinborg's remarkable journey through life. A short biography, which highlights the nature of her character and personality, has been included at the end of this book.

Readers will find significant parallels between the author's life and the lives of her main characters'. Names and events are fictitious, but the story provides a window into parts of Icelandic society during the 1920s. The main characters in this play are ordinary people who go about their everyday lives until "one's future is all smashed up, for no fault" of one's own and the ship has to steer into a new direction, to quote Elsa in the play.

All proceeds of this book will be donated to Speranta Terrei. Speranta Terrei is a community organisation in Balti, in northern Moldova, raising awareness and treating TB and HIV patients and supports families throughout the community. Since 2022, Speranta Terrei has been supporting hundreds of additional families of displaced Ukrainians. They are a little-known charity worthy of our support: https://www.globalgiving.org/donate/5666/speranta-terrei/

Iris E Ferrier and James McD Ferrier (grandson)
March 2023

WHY THE CAPTAIN DID NOT MARRY

GUÐBJÖRG ELINBORG ÞÓRÐARDÓTTIR

Born: 8 August 1908, Isafjord, Iceland

Died: 4 July 1983, London, England

WHY THE CAPTAIN DID NOT MARRY

CHARACTERS

ALFRED EIRIKSSON, (the skipper)	Age abt. 47,	tall, fair hair
MARIE, (his wife)	Age abt. 43,	medium, brown hair
KNUD, (their son)	Age abt. 15,	medium, brown hair
ANNA, (their only daughter)	Age abt. 8,	tall, fair hair
EMIL, (their younger son)	Age abt. 4,	fair hair
HANSEN, (the boat owner)	Age abt. 43	small, dark hair
PETERSEN, (boat-agent and merchant)	Age abt. 38	medium, brown hair
HENDRIKSEN, (the bar owner)	Age abt. 50	tall, brown hair
KAROLINA BJORNSSON, (a widow)	Age abt.52	medium, fair hair
NANNA, (her daughter)	Age abt. 12	medium, fair hair
HALFDAN & BROTHER, (the two fishermen)	Age abt. 45	medium, brown hair
ANNA JONSSON, (a widow)	Age abt. 53	small, brown hair
MARGRJET, (her daughter)	Age abt. 30	tall, fair hair

ELSA HANSEN, (MARGRJET's daughter)	Age abt. 16	medium, fair hair
OSWALD HANSEN, (later MARGRJET's husband)	Age abt. 35	tall, brown hair
EMIL ALFREDSSON, (as a young man)	Age abt. 19-30	tall, fair hair
ARNI SIGURDSSON, (THE MESS BOY)	Age abt. 21	tall, dark hair
ELSA HANSEN'S 3 GIRLFRIENDS		
BAR-MAN		
TWO DANISH GENTLEMEN		
LANDLADY		
MRS. HAMPTON	Age abt. 48	medium, brown hair
MR. HAMPTON	Age abt. 52	tall, dark hair
MR. AND MRS. BURTON AND SON		
CAPTAIN SIGURGEIRSSON	Age abt. 55	tall, dark hair
THE BOY FRIENDS OF EMIL		

BOLUNGARVIK

It is in the small fishing village on the west coast of Iceland called Bolungarvik, that a motorboat is landing, and as soon as it is fastened to the little wooden pier, the skipper ALFRED EIRIKSSON, is ashore, and goes straight to the office of MR. HANSEN, who owns the boat, as well as three other similar boats.

HANSEN   [*sitting behind a desk in his small office, looking up from his bookkeeping as the door opens, looking straight into the skipper's eyes*] ALFRED, I have been receiving bills for food that seem a little too high, what I mean is, that there are items on them that I do not think absolutely necessary.

ALFRED   Well, it may be that you do not think it necessary, but I do, [*in a louder voice*] my men work hard, and we cannot just live on fish and old rotten potatoes.

HANSEN, who could not afford to lose his best skipper, always bringing in the best catch, thinks he would be wiser not to argue the matter any further, and just hands the skipper a receipt to sign, and then hands him the money due to him. Although he knows most of it would go to the local bar, as ALFRED's custom was to go there first, before going home.

This time, however, ALFRED goes straight home, just stopping to greet an old friend who is coming out of the bar as he passes.

MARIE   [*seeing him enter the kitchen of the small house they live in, is quite startled, for usually, at least an hour elapses from the time he lands till the time he comes to the house, and then he is not always in the best of mood. She looks at him quite frightenedly and says in a low voice, so as not to raise his anger*] ALFRED are you not feeling well, or what has happened?

ALFRED   [*before answering, he throws his bag into a corner, takes his cap off and sits down*] No, I am very well, only HANSEN cannot do anything better than greet me with complaints every time I land.

MARIE   Never mind dear, you will be your own master someday, so don't you worry. I will have your cup of tea ready in few minutes; I am just baking a few pancakes for you. I would have had them done, but I did not expect you quite so early. [*calling*] ANNA, go and get your father a bottle of beer from the pantry. [*to ALFRED*] I bought two bottles just to keep in the house, and you look tired so you might as well have one just now as the tea is not ready.

[ANNA *enters with a bottle of beer.*]

MARIE   No ANNA don't give it to your father in the bottle. Bring him a tumbler.

ALFRED	[*Although not saying so,* ALFRED *is really glad of his wife's thoughtfulness, having a bottle of beer for him in the house. After drinking the glass of beer, he feels better and becomes more talkative, and is full of what he intends to do in the future.*] I am going to have a boat of my own, and not have that old fool nagging me about something or other, every time I land. After I leave, we will see what his annual profit will be. I know he can get plenty of chaps to take the boat, but I am not so sure they bring in the catch as I do every time. Nor will they ever know the fishing banks as I do.
MARIE	That is right ALFRED, you will get a boat of your own shortly, but you will have to start putting some money aside, every week, so that you can pay at least a part in the boat when you get it. Otherwise, the interest alone will be too much.
ALFRED	I am going to see about a boat right now, when I finish my tea. Leave some shaving water ready for me, will you, and take out my blue suit.
MARIE	Whom are you going to see ALFRED about a boat?
ALFRED	I think I will see MR. PETERSEN first. His boats are the best, and I think his terms are quite reasonable, at least I will hear what they are.
MARIE	Yes, ALFRED, you can hear what he says. He might even want you to start a business with him.

ALFRED	I am not going to start any business with anybody, I am going to start on my own, and have all the responsibility of it myself.
MARIE	But remember ALFRED, if there is a loss the burden would not be so heavy for you.
ALFRED	So that is what you think. But what about the profit? I have always been the luckiest skipper, and I fail to see why that should change if I was working for my own benefit.

ALFRED *after finishing his tea, rests for a little while.* MARIE, *however, uses the opportunity to walk down to* MR. PETERSEN's *office, to put in a good word for her husband, although she is doubtful about* ALFRED's *success as his own boss, for he has never been careful with money. Nonetheless, she is not going to stand in his way; at least, he is entitled to try, and if he needed, she herself has saved a little money which she could lend him to get over the difficulties this coming season. So occupied is she with her own thoughts, that she has already walked past* MR. PETERSEN's *office. She turns back, knocks on the door at his office, and she can hear the loud voice of* MR. PETERSEN *himself.*

PETERSEN	Come in.
MARIE	[*opens the door and steps in quickly*] Good afternoon, MR. PETERSEN.
PETERSEN	Good afternoon, MRS. EIRIKSSON, this is indeed a surprise to have a visit from you. And what can I do for you? [*looking straight into her face.*]

MARIE	[*tells him about her husband's intentions and adds that she herself had some money, which if it came to the worst, she would willingly pay for him, but that she of course hopes that the venture would prove a profitable one*] Our son KNUD is now old enough to help his father, and he has always wanted to go to sea, so I think he might make good, although it is not my wish that he shall become a sailor.
PETERSEN	MRS. EIRIKSSON, I shall be glad to do all I can for your husband, and I feel sure we will come to some arrangements that will suit both of us.
MARIE	Thank you, MR. PETERSEN, I will be hurrying away now, so good-bye.
PETERSEN	Good-bye MRS. EIRIKSSON.

MARIE *returns home, opens the kitchen door carefully, takes her coat and hat off, and busies herself in the kitchen so that* ALFRED *would not know that she has been out. She is just putting on the kettle to make herself a cup of tea, when* ALFRED *comes into the kitchen.*

ALFRED	I am going out now and will be back shortly. Oh, MARIE, where is my bank book? I have perhaps better take it with me, I might have to show it to MR. PETERSEN.
MARIE	Yes ALFRED, I will get it for you. Here it is. Good luck. [*kisses him*].

5

ALFRED	[*walks quickly to reach* MR. PETERSEN*'s office before closing time. He knocks and before hearing any answer, opens the door and walks in.*] Good afternoon, MR. PETERSEN.
PETERSEN	Good afternoon, and what can I do for you MR. EIRIKSSON? Please take a seat, I am just decoding a telegram, I won't keep you a minute. I hope your boat, that is to say the motor, is giving satisfaction.
ALFRED	Oh yes, indeed it is, what I really came to see you about, was whether we could not come to some agreement regarding a purchase of a new motor-boat for myself. The trouble is that I can only pay a small sum outright just now, and of course not too high monthly instalments either. So, what are your terms? I would like to hear them MR. PETERSEN, if you don't mind. I am sorry being so late.
PETERSEN	The terms are very reasonable. Of course, the first payment is a little heavy. How much can you pay down?
ALFRED	Well, about £120 to £130.
PETERSEN	I dare say that will be alright, and how much can you manage each month after that?
ALFRED	That is just it, MR. PETERSEN, you see that is a little unsettled; it depends largely upon how the fishing goes, but I think it is safe to say £15 to £20 and perhaps £30 during the fishing season.

PETERSEN	I would like to make it as easy as possible for you MR. EIRIKSSON, but I have my orders. So, if you could make it say £25 per month just now and £40 per month during the season, I can very probably press them to accept it. And what about the delivery, when do you want the boat?
ALFRED	As soon as possible.
PETERSEN	Very well, MR. EIRIKSSON, I will send the telegram tonight, and let you know the answer and the price as soon as I get it.
ALFRED	Thank you very much MR. PETERSEN, and I should like you not to mention this to anybody.
PETERSEN	Certainly not, and I will draw up the contract and have it ready for you to sign, immediately after I receive their answer.
ALFRED	That is fine, I hope everything will be fixed before I leave in two days.
PETERSEN	Oh yes, they are usually very prompt.
ALFRED	Good afternoon, MR. PETERSEN. I am sorry having kept you after closing hour.
PETERSEN	That is quite alright. Good afternoon.

ALFRED *hurries home. He is very happy, for he knows that* PETERSEN *would press the firm to agree to the terms, for he has not sold many boats during this winter, and he is only working on commission.*

| MARIE | [*seeing how happy he looks, she walks towards him*] Well Captain, when is the boat sailing? |
| ALFRED | [*answers in an unusually good tone*] Within two months, Madam. |

TWO DAYS LATER

ALFRED *does not go much out during the two next days, but instead spends most of the time calculating how much money it would be possible for him to make, reckoning with the same luck as he had hitherto had with his catch. Then for the first time, he sees how impossible it is for him to ask* MR. HANSEN *to buy his catch, as he is the only one in the village who has a curing station and sells the fish through an agent in Reykjavik to Spain.*

ALFRED	[*calls*] MARIE come here for a minute, will you?
MARIE	What is it ALFRED? I am just coming.
ALFRED	I have just been thinking, that it is not possible for me to sell my fish to HANSEN, and that means that I will have to go to another port each time I land to sell my catch.
MARIE	[*who does not like to disappoint* ALFRED *in his happy mood, is quick to reply*] But we could sell the house and move to a place where you could sell the fish. After all, your home must be where you land your catch. But I hope it will not have to be far away from here, for after all these years here, we are sure to miss the place and our old friends. But I dare say we would soon get over that. To start with we could just rent three rooms and a kitchen, and then later, if everything goes well, we could perhaps buy a small house again.

ALFRED *looks at* MARIE *and listens to her with keen interest.*

MARIE	Anyway, don't you worry, we will be alright. And of course, ALFRED, you will take KNUD with you on the new boat. I am sure he will be a good help for you, which means you will have to pay less money out for deck hands.
ALFRED	Well, I had thought of that, only I did not like to suggest it to you, as I knew you don't really want him to become a sailor. But seeing you are not against him helping me, I feel sure he will like to come. However, I think it best not to say anything to the children about this just yet, until we are quite fixed. MARIE, are you quite sure MR. PETERSEN did not send a message to me while I was out today?
MARIE	Oh, quite sure ALFRED.

ALFRED *has hardly finished his sentence, when looking through the window he sees* MR. PETERSEN *himself coming towards the house, carrying a large envelope in his hand.*

MARIE	ALFRED put on your jacket, quick, MR. PETERSEN is here now.
ALFRED	[*does not wait for* MR. PETERSEN *to knock, but goes to the door and opens it*] I am indeed pleased to see you MR. PETERSEN, come right in and take a seat.

9

PETERSEN   Thank you. Well, I have the telegram here, and they have accepted the terms, except the first payment, which they say, must be at least £150.00, but the monthly payments as we had agreed to, and of course I hope you can see your way to accept this; I am sorry, but that is how it is.

ALFRED   [*thoughtful for a moment, then he rises sharply to his feet*] Yes, I will manage that somehow, so please tell them to have it ready for delivery as soon as possible. I will just read the contract over before I sign it, if you don't mind.

PETERSEN   Certainly, and of course as you know, all this is just a matter of form, I have underlined everything that really matters.

MARIE   [*comes into the room, carrying a tray with coffee, etc.*] I hope I am not disturbing you, I have just brought in some coffee, thought you might like to have a cup with us MR. PETERSEN. I have just made some fresh pancakes, which I am sure you will like, at least ALFRED does.

PETERSEN   Thank you I will accept your kind offer, and as for pancakes, they are the very best I get with coffee, so I am quite sure I will like them.

ALFRED   [*handing two copies of the contract to MR. PETERSEN, carefully folding the copy he is to keep himself*] Well here you are, and I hope this is only the beginning and that I will be buying more boats from you in the near future.

PETERSEN   [*after putting the copies back into the large envelope, rises*] Thank you both for the coffee and the extremely nice pancakes, no wonder MR. EIRIKSSON likes them. Well, I hope you will do well MR. EIRIKSSON and buy a few of my boats. Good afternoon to you, and I hope you have a good trip MR. EIRIKSSON. [*leaving*]

MARIE   Now that all this is settled, you should really go and have a nice rest, as you will have to get up early in the morning.

ALFRED   Yes dear, I am going to lie down until, dinner, and then I might go down and see some of the old fellows.

MARIE   That is right ALFRED, but remember you need all your cash, so don't spend too much.

ALFRED   Don't you worry about that, this time I am not going to spend any money at all.

After dinner ALFRED *goes to the bar; his friends come quickly round him, to ask, why he has not been to see them since he landed. They expect that* ALFRED *would get angry, but he is too happy this time, so instead he answers them good humouredly.*

ALFRED   My dear boys, do you really think it absolutely necessary to come here every time, for if you do, you are wrong. When I have other things to attend to, I do that first.

ONE OF THE BOVS   Oh, you have been transacting some big business, that is fine.

11

ALFRED *goes straight to the bar-man, and asks if he could see the manager.*

BAR-MAN	Yes Sir, go right into the office, you will find MR. HENDRIKSEN there.
HENDRIKSEN	[*sitting behind his desk*] This is a pleasure. What can I do for you MR. EIRIKSSON?
ALFRED	Good evening, I just came to see, if some of the money I owe you, can be paid in three months' time or so, instead of next month, as I have a great deal to pay out next month.
HENDRIKSEN	Of course, of course, for an old friend and customer like you, I will do anything I can, so I will just have a look at your account. Yes, here it is, £3.18.6. up to date.
ALFRED	Alright, I will pay the 18/6 just now and leave the £3, if I may.
HENDRIKSEN	Yes, certainly that is quite alright.
ALFRED	Thank you MR. HENDRIKSEN. I will not be seeing you for the next few days, as I am leaving in the morning, so good-bye.
HENDRIKSEN	Well, I hope you have a good trip, and the same luck as usual.
ALFRED	I will, goodbye.

When ALFRED *comes downstairs, he orders a glass of beer, for which he pays by cash. He takes It over to a table where his friends sit; they are in a serious discussion about everything that has taken place since their last meeting, and after a few minutes he leaves them to go home.*

MARIE   [*just getting* ALFRED's *clothes ready for the morning; the children are already in bed. She is glad to see him come home sober, and murmurs to herself*] God has heard my prayers at last, and made ALFRED give up drinking. Now I know he will do well, and be a man amongst men.

The alarm-clock rings at five o'clock in the morning, so up they get quickly, for the boat has to leave at six o'clock.

MARIE *goes to the kitchen and puts the kettle on first of all. Then she has another look at* ALFRED's *bag to see if everything he will need is there. Yes, she has put everything in except his cake-tin, which now is ready to go in the bag as well. Now the kettle is boiling, she makes a pot of tea, and they each drink a cup in a hurry, then* MARIE *takes her coat and hat and goes down to the boat with* ALFRED *to bid him good-bye and good luck.*

MARIE *cannot help the tears rolling down her cheeks as she kisses* ALFRED *farewell; she has always been like that from the very first. She hurries home as soon as the boat has left, to see to the children's breakfast, before they go to school. This time somehow or other she feels as if she has been saying good-bye for the last time. Then she thinks, how silly of me. It is just because* ALFRED *has been more at home this time, and different from what he has been for a long time. As soon as she enters the house, she takes off her coat and hat, runs upstairs to call to the children that it is time to get up. They get up, eat their breakfast and go off to school.*

THE NEXT MORNING

Next morning, the weather is dull, and at noon the wind is getting very strong, so it is no wonder that the women are getting anxious, for they know too well the danger this might bring their husbands and sons who are out at sea. So now, practically every few minutes, you can see in most of the houses a face of a woman anxiously looking towards the sea hoping to see the little boats hurrying towards land.

However, it is not till late in the afternoon that the first boats come in, and the wives run down to the shore to welcome their husbands. Towards evening the storm gets worse and worse, and no more boats come in, so people start to get worried about their safety.

At last, one more boat comes into view. Now the big question is, who is it? It is indeed a hard struggle for a rowing boat. Oh yes, it is now well in sight. It is OLD HALFDAN and his brother. Well, here they are at last. Several men come to help them pull the boat up. They have practically no fish; the sea has swept it back again.

HALFDAN	Well folk, this is going to be some storm, and we have not seen the worst of it yet. [*then turning to* MR. HANSEN, *who is amongst the people standing nearby*] HANSEN, I hope we are the last to land. Are all the boats in?
HANSEN	No, unfortunately not, there are three rowing boats and five motor-boats out yet, unless they have gone into another harbour for shelter.

HALFDAN	That is funny. We did not see any of them. We only saw a trawler, and I rather think it was a foreigner. It was drawing in its gear. When did the skipper leave MR. HANSEN?
HANSEN	Six o'clock yesterday morning. He may be not so far out, although we cannot see them, for the mist is very thick.
HALFDAN	I hope so, for this is going to be no joke. He should get into harbour wherever he is.

There is great excitement in the little village during the evening. The storm is quite the worst for many years, and none of the three boats missing have yet landed. Telephone communication between the villages is impossible, as the wires have broken down, so news about their safety would not reach them until the mail-boat arrives, which is not till after three or four days.

THE FOURTH DAY

This is the fourth day. The storm has at last ceased and the sea is calming down to its normal again. The mail-boat is expected in the afternoon, and as nothing has been heard from the missing boats, people are anxiously awaiting its arrival, for this was the only hope relatives have left to hear that the boats have managed to get into other harbours for shelter.

The mail-boat is an hour and a half late. Yes, there is half a sack of letters and papers for Bolungarvik, so the women and some of the men follow the man who carries the bag to the post-office. The shop-keeper opens the bag and hands out in silence the letters and papers to their owners. Most of the women get letters, however, there are two wives and one mother who get no letters, so their hope of some news of their husbands and son, now vanishes for they know there is no hope of these small boats still being above water.

MARIE   [*having her letter in her hand still unopened, goes over where the three women are standing; she addresses* CAROLINA *(the widow) who has lost her husband seven years ago, and now her son has gone as well, so all she has left is a little girl of twelve*] I will walk home with you CAROLINA.

MARIE *comforts her as best she can, and it falls to her to tell the sad news to little* NANNA, *who is just coming home from school.*

NANNA   I cannot believe this, for God has always heard my prayers, and I have prayed every night that my brother might come home again, and I know God would not take him away from mother and me.

MARIE *kisses* CAROLINA *and tells her she would now have to leave. She also kisses* NANNA. *Then she goes straight home, with her own letter clasped tight in her right hand. She is in deep thoughts on the way home. Then she looks at the letter in her hand and says aloud to herself*] Thank God ALFRED is alive, for there is no doubt about that this is his handwriting on the envelope. [*then her thoughts wander back to* CAROLINA *and* NANNA. *Could It be possible that God had taken* BJÖRN *away from them in the prime of his life? Only about 18 he was, and their only support. She hurries into the house; the children are already home from school and they immediately ask if there is news of their father.*

MARIE   Yes, but I have not read the letter yet. ANNA, you put on the kettle and make some tea, and KNUD you can help ANNA set the table. She opens the letter, which is as follows and reads it quietly.

Dear MARIE,

The boat stranded on a reef outside Hnifsdalur but fortunately all hands were saved.

As I was the last to leave the boat, I happened to fall and break my left leg, but the boat that took us to Isafjord had a doctor onboard, so he was able to help me right away, which of course made a great difference. I am now lying in a private house, as the hospital was full up. It is a house, which belongs to a widow and her daughter. They are both extremely kind to me, but I am afraid I shall not be able to walk for a month or two yet, as my leg was very badly broken.

I will be writing shortly again. With love to the children and yourself, ALFRED.

P.S. I have heard the sad news about the loss of lives so I count myself very lucky to get away with only a broken leg.

MARIE [*after reading the letter sits thinking, and then saying aloud to herself*] Poor ALFRED, so he broke his leg, that was hard luck, but still, I can thank God that he is still alive. So, I have no right to grumble. [*She calls to the children and tells them of their father's accident. They all sit down to drink their tea, and are all very silent. Suddenly their big cat comes into the room and goes straight to EMIL, the youngest. EMIL starts at once telling the pussy about his father's accident, and adds how father will have to walk with a big stick, like the rich people do. The others glance at each other and cannot help smiling.*

After clearing the table, the children settle down to do their homework and MARIE *sits down to write to* ALFRED. *She tells him the news from the village. She further tells him not to worry about her or the children, and to take good care of himself and not start walking too soon.*

HNIFSDALUR – FOUR MONTHS LATER

ALFRED *has been getting on fine;* MARGRJET, *the daughter has been doing all the nursing, and they have become very good friends. As a matter of fact, they are in love, although* MARGRJET *is only about 30, but* ALFRED 47.

MARIE *does not receive many letters from* ALFRED *and in none of those she has received, has he mentioned when he was coming home. Now it is over four months since his accident has happened.*

ALFRED is *having his breakfast with* MARGRJET, *when the post brings him a letter from* MARIE *and in it another letter from* MR. PETERSEN, *saying that the boat is ready for delivery and that the firm has sent a telegram, asking for the first payment. This seems to rouse* ALFRED *from his slumber and sets him thinking, and he decides that he will have to tell* MARGRJET *that he will have to go back home at once, although he feels as if this house has become his home.*

They have dinner at twelve o'clock as usual. While they are eating, ALFRED *tells* MARGRJET *about the content of the letters and that he will have to go.*

MARGRJET   Well, there is not much I can say or do to stop you from going back to your home, although, I am sorry and I know I will miss you very much.

ALFRED	But MARGRJET dear, you know I would not go so soon, but this is very important, and as you know I will be coming back as soon as I possibly can again.
MARGRJET	[*rises to her feet*] But ALFRED, there is something I must tell you.
ALFRED	What is it dear? You look so sad.
MARGRJET	It seems so terrible to have to tell you, but I am going to have a baby.
ALFRED	What, a baby?
MARGRJET	[*crying*] Yes, aren't you glad? You know we love each other. So now that I cannot see you, I will have somebody to care for and love.
ALFRED	Of course, dear, but you know this must simply not be known, at least not that I am the father, as it would break MARIE's heart, and there are also my children to be considered.
MARGRJET	I know darling, but I had to tell you.
ALFRED	We will think of some way out, but I will have to go back by the first boat. But don't you worry, I will be able to send you some money, as I firmly believe that my new boat will do well. But as for the baby's name, it will have to bear some other name than mine, say, it could be christened HANSEN. That is equally suitable for a boy or a girl; then the baby's real surname would not have to be known. How do you like my idea MARGRJET?

MARGRJET   I think the idea is very good, but what really worries me is to have to stay in this place, where everybody knows everybody, and all the gossip.

ALFRED   But what about going away to some place till it is all over, and then bring the baby home. I am sure your mother would not mind a baby in the house, and of course she will know who the real father is, but I know she will understand the circumstances.

MARGRJET   Say, you must have thought all this out beforehand. It is just as if you have planned such a speech, long ago. Or have you had other experiences like this before?

ALFRED   Why do you say such a thing MARGRJET? I am only trying to do the best, and as to thinking things out quickly, I am used to having to take decisions at once, so my brain acts quickly. [pauses and walks over to MARGRJET] Well my dear, I am just going out now to see when the next boat leaves, but remember, you are not to worry about anything. Everything is going to be alright.

MARGRJET   It is all very well, not to worry, but besides people looking down on girls who have babies without being married, there Is also the expense to be considered. However, I am not worrying, at least not yet. So, you go along and see about the boat, and don't be long now.

ALFRED   No, I won't be long. [*kisses her, takes his hat and goes out*]

When ALFRED *comes down to the harbour, he is told there is a boat leaving in two hours' time for Bolungarvik, and that there would not be another boat to Bolungarvik for about three days. He decides there and then that he would have to take the boat leaving in two hours. So, he hurries back home to* MARGRJET *to tell her the news, and to spend what little time he has left with her. However, he thinks it better to go upstairs first and pack his bag. Having done so he goes downstairs.*

ALFRED   [*raises his voice as he cannot see* MARGRJET] MARGRJET, MARGRJET.

No answer, so he sits down. Then MRS. JONSSON, MARGRJET'*s mother, comes in to see what* ALFRED *wants.*

MRS. JONSSON   Anything I can do for you, ALFRED?

ALFRED   I am leaving in less than two hours' time, so if you will kindly tell me how much I owe you. I would like to settle with you, before I leave. I am sorry to be leaving, you have been awfully kind to me.

MRS. JONSSON   Oh, you really owe us nothing, ALFRED. We have been more than pleased to have you, and you have really been no trouble at all.

23

As they are standing there talking, MARGRJET *comes in. She has been out shopping, so she goes first to the kitchen, before joining them.*

MARGRJET	Tell, tell me all the news. Is there any boat today?
ALFRED	Yes, there is a boat leaving just in an hour and three quarters' time, so there is not much time left.
MRS. JONSSON	I will go and put on the kettle. I am sure ALFRED would like a cup of coffee before he leaves.
ALFRED	Thank you. It is awfully kind of you.
MARGRJET	That is right mother; I will come and help you get it ready [*turning to* ALFRED] I won't be long; you sit down till I come.
ALFRED	Right, I will do that [*he walks into the dining-room, takes a book out of the bookcase, and sits down. He does not open the book, but sits thinking deeply, and looks round the room, as if he is trying to memorise every little thing that is in the room. He buries his head in his hands, and just then* MARGRJET *enters the room, with a little tray with coffee and cakes on it;* ALFRED *looks up.*] Hello darling, at last you are here. These few minutes have been like an hour.
MARGRJET	I tried to be as quick as I possibly could, for there is only an hour of so left.

ALFRED   I know MARGRJET dear, but I really don't
              feel as if this is good-bye, I am sure we will
              see each other very soon again. You
              know, that, very likely, I will be bringing
              my catch in here to sell, so you will have
              me as a regular visitor every week. At
              least, I hope so. I will write and let you
              know my plans as soon as possible

MARGRJET   ALFRED, I was thinking over, what you
              said this morning about me going away. I
              really think it would be the best thing to
              do. Mother has always wanted me to go
              to Reykjavik. So now I am going to take
              the opportunity.

ALFRED   Yes, I think that would be the best, but
              then I cannot see you, even if I come to
              sell my catch here.

MARGRJET   No, but perhaps that is just as well; you
              will have to forget me anyway.

ALFRED   I am afraid that is going to be a very
              difficult job for me, as you are all the time
              in my thoughts.

MARGRJET   It will not be so easy for me either to
              forget you ALFRED. You have been very
              kind to us, and we will both miss you.

ALFRED   Nonsense, you and your mother have
              been more than kind to me, and I would
              not have got on so well, if it had not been
              for you darling, and what hurts me most
              is to have to leave you like this, after
              having put a stain on your character.
              [ALFRED *moves closer to* MARGRJET *and
              puts his arms round her, their eyes meet
              and they kiss*]

25

[*The old clock on the wall chimes two, so their time together is up.* ALFRED *rises, and* MARGRJET *wipes the tears from her eyes, and also stands up.*]

ALFRED	Well, my dear, I will have to get going; so, I will get my things downstairs and say good-bye to your mother. You stay here till I come back.
MARGRJET	I will be here. I am just going to put these things away to the kitchen.

ALFRED *comes back in two minutes' time with his sailor sack on his back.* MARGRJET *is standing, looking out of the window, but as* ALFRED *enters the room, she walks towards him. He takes her in his arms and they kiss.*

ALFRED	Well dear, this is just a good-bye for the present, so don't look so sad; you know love always finds a way.
MARGRJET	So, they say, but you also love your wife. So, it will be difficult to serve two masters and be true to both, you know. So, I think that this is really a parting.
ALFRED	That is very true. I love my wife and she has always been a good wife and mother, and I would not do anything to hurt her feelings, but falling in love is a thing one cannot help, but anyway it is too late now, and to tell you the truth I really don't regret is. We have had such a wonderful time together.
MARGRJET	Well, you must go now, or you will miss the boat.

Once more they kiss; then ALFRED *hurries away, but* MARGRJET *goes to the window to wave him a last good-bye, and stands looking out of the window as long as he is in sight.*

When ALFRED *passes the telegraph office, he suddenly remembers that he has not sent his wife a telegram to tell, her when to expect him home. So, he goes in and writes out a telegram, hands it to the girl, and pays for it.*

BOLUNGARVIK

MARIE *is busy washing, when the telegram arrives. But after knowing that* ALFRED *would be home in less than three hours' time, she decides to leave the rest and to start baking some of* ALFRED's *favourite cakes. When her baking is done, she goes upstairs to change. Somehow or other, she feels she has to look her best. So, she takes out the old iron tongues, which she heats. Then she curls the tops of her hair. This done, she puts the kettle on in readiness for their homecoming, so that* ALFRED *would not have to wait long for his coffee. She goes to the window; yes, the boat is almost at the pier now, she will have to hurry.*

ALFRED   [*is already on the pier when she arrives there; he then realises how glad he is to see her again. He flings his arms round* MARIE *and kisses her*] How glad I am to see you and be back home again.

MARIE   [*looks into* ALFRED's *eyes, and without saving so, thinks he has changed*] I am glad to see you back ALFRED, and you are really looking well, and that is more important.

ALFRED   Yes, I am looking well, and no wonder, the two women, with whom I stayed, looked after me wonderfully. In fact, they were far too good to me, and I would not have got on so well if it had not been for their very good care.

MARIE   I am glad to hear that.

As they were walking away, MR. HANSEN *and two other men came to see* ALFRED.

HANSEN	Welcome back Alfred, and how are you feeling?
ALFRED	I am feeling fine, thank you.
HANSEN	Could you come and see me tomorrow morning? There are few things, regarding the old boat, that I should like to discuss with you.
ALFRED	Yes, I will come to the office tomorrow morning, about 10 o'clock, will that suit you?
HANSEN	Make it 10.30, if you don't mind.
ALFRED	That suits me, bye-bye.
MARIE	The children will be surprised, when you are home, as they had just left for school after lunch, when your telegram came. Oh, while I remember, I expect MR. PETERSEN will be coming to see you, as soon as he knows you are here. He is quite excited about the boat, and wants you to take delivery as soon as possible.
ALFRED	So am I, MARIE, believe me. It is a fine feeling to know that I am going to be my own master after all these years.
MARIE	I am sure it is, and I only hope that you will be happy and as lucky as you always have been.
ALFRED	Don't you worry. You will see, and very shortly too.

They have reached the house by now.

MARIE   The kettle is boiling now, so I will make the coffee. You sit down and rest.

ALFRED   That is fine, I am very hungry; so, don't keep me waiting long.

Just as they have finished drinking the coffee, there is a knock at the door.

ALFRED   Come in.

MARIE   Who can that be?

The door opens and in comes Mr. PETERSEN.

PETERSEN   Good afternoon, and I hope you will excuse me for coming to disturb you, just as you are coming home. But I had to see you.

ALFRED   Not at all, come right in and take a seat MR. PETERSEN, I am very glad to see you, and I am really anxious to get the boat at once. I am really feeling that I have been staying too long on land, and quite missing the sea. So, when do you think we can have it here?

PETERSEN   If I sent them a telegram right now that you want the boat delivered at once, they should be able to have it delivered to you here in less than a week's time.

ALFRED   That is splendid, and I expect you want the first payment before sending the telegram.

PETERSEN   Well, that is the rule you know.

ALFRED   Now let me see, well I know, I will give you my bank-book just now, and then we can go and draw out the money in the morning, if that is O.K. with you?

PETERSEN   It certainly is O.K. with me, but is it not asking too much?

ALFRED   No, not at all, I want the boat. [*goes to a chest of drawers to get the book*] Here you are MR. PETERSEN. [*hands him the book*]

PETERSEN   Thank you very much indeed MR. EIRIKSSON, I will send the telegram immediately. So good-bye, see you in the morning. [*puts on his hat, and walks quickly to the telegraph office, as the telegram is already to be sent*]

ALFRED *is very restless during the night and cannot sleep. He keeps thinking about* MARGRJET; *if only he had not left her in this condition, he could be happy. For* MARGRJET *is still young, and would soon have forgotten him, but with having the baby it will be more difficult. What can he do? He cannot possibly tell* MARIE. *So, the best would be to leave it at least for the time being.*

ALFRED *is up early, he shaves, has his breakfast, then leaves the house right away to see* MR. PETERSEN, *for he will have to be by 10.30 at* MR. HANSEN's *office.*

ONE WEEK LATER

It is just a week since ALFRED's *arrival home, and his new boat is due to arrive any moment. He looks out of the window to see, if there is any sign of it already, but no, so far there is no sign of it coming.* MARIE *is just as excited; she cannot settle down to her work. Just as* ALFRED *and* MARIE *are both standing at the window,* KNUD *comes rushing in full of excitement.*

KNUD	Father, the boat is coming. When I passed MR. PETERSEN's office, he was looking through his binoculars, and said that he could see a boat coming, and that it could only be your new boat.
ALFRED	Oh good, KNUD. MARIE hurry up. Let us all go down to the pier. It will be here in less than ten minutes time.
MARIE	I won't be long Alfred.
ALFRED	[*still looking out of the window*] Here she is and what a beauty, and she is going smoothly. MARIE are you ready, for it will be at the pier in less than three minutes' time now.
MARIE	Yes, I am just coming!

They walk quickly to the pier. MR. PETERSEN *is already there, introducing himself and exchanging greetings with* TWO DANISH GENTLEMEN *onboard.*

PETERSEN	[*as soon as* ALFRED *comes, he calls to the* TWO DANISH GENTLEMEN] This is MR. EIRIKSSON who is buying the boat, his wife and son.

TWO   How do you do, pleased to meet you.
DANISH
GENTLEMEN

MARIE *and* KNUD *nod and* ALFRED *lifts his hat to them.* Now the boat is properly fastened to the pier, MR. PETERSEN, ALFRED, KNUD *and* MARIE all go onboard to have a good look round the new boat, which they all admire very much. After discussing few new improvements etc., MR. PETERSEN asks them all to come to his house and have coffee with him.

The men are all very gay, but MARIE *being the only woman present, is rather shy and quiet, except when she has an opportunity to exchange few words with* MR. PETERSEN's *housekeeper, when she is bringing some things for the table.*

The TWO DANISH GENTLEMEN, *ask* ALFRED *to come down to the boat with them, as they wanted to show him the chart of the boat and go into details with him.*

THE FOLLOWING DAYS

The following day, ALFRED *is very busy, signing his men on, ordering the provisions etc. for he is setting off in two or three days' time.*

KNUD *is very excited, for he is to go with his father for the first time.*

MARIE *is also very busy getting everything ready for them both.*

The morning they have decided to leave is glorious, and promptly at five o'clock they are off. And even then, being so early in the morning, MARIE *has come down to the pier with her husband and son to see them off. And when the boat is no longer in sight, she hurries to her home, now and then, drying the tears that are rolling down her cheeks.*

ALFRED	[*sitting in his nice and clean cabin*] KNUD come here a minute.
KNUD	[*standing just outside his father's door*] Yes Father, what is it?
ALFRED	Was there any letter for me by the mail-boat yesterday?
KNUD	I don't think so Father.
ALFRED	That is alright, Son. I thought perhaps your mother had forgotten to tell me, as we were all so excited. [*then talking to himself*] Why has not MARGRJET written, I wonder, perhaps she has been too busy?

ALFRED *is very lucky during the fishing season, so he is doing splendidly for himself. He is able to sell all his catch to a fish merchant at Hnifsdalur. So, it saves him a lot of time, instead of having to go to Isafjord, as he at first has thought. And as for the drinking, he has not tasted wine or beer. So, he is really an altogether different man. Every time he comes to Bolungarvik, he asks, if there has been any letter for him, but no,* MARGRJET *has not written him a line since he has left Isafjord.*

MARGRJET

MARGRJET *is in Reykjavik; she has been working very hard as a help in a hotel laundry, and now she is giving up her job to prepare for her big event. She has booked a bed in the hospital in a fortnight's time. However, on returning home in the evening, she thinks she feels awfully funny, so she asks the Landlady, if she would be kind enough to get her a taxi. The Landlady telephones for the taxi, and it is at the door in a few minutes' time.* MARGRJET *tells the Landlady that she is going to the hospital, as she is not feeling too well. The Landlady wishes her the best of luck.*

MARGRJET *drives straight to the hospital. She asks, if she were able to stay the night there, as she is not feeling well.*

She is allowed to do so. Her decision to go to the hospital has indeed been wise, for after only few hours, her baby is born, a little girl, 6-3/4 lbs. A telegram is sent to her mother telling her the news. The Old Lady is very pleased as she has wanted the baby to be a girl.

MARGRJET *has made arrangements that the Landlady should take care of the baby during the day-time, so that she could go out to work again, as she does not want to go to Isafjord just yet.* MARGRJET *is able to get her old job in the hotel laundry back, and is very happy although sometimes very tired, for very often she has not had much sleep during the night with the baby. However, she feels that she has something to live for and work for, and that makes her very proud and happy.*

THREE YEARS LATER

Just three years later, on the little girl's third birthday, MARGRJET *is giving a little party to celebrate the day. There is of course the Landlady, three men who also live in the house and have always been very kind to little* ELSA *(that was the girls' name), and two girls from the hotel laundry.*

Little ELSA *is allowed to stay up a little longer than usual, so that she might be able to have some of her birthday cake. Ever since that cake was put on the table little* ELSA *had been walking round the table. There are three candles on the cake and further in the centre is the name* ELSA HANSEN, *for the girl had been christened* HANSEN.

One of the men present OSWALD HANSEN, *rises to help little* ELSA *cut the cake, and when he notices the name* HANSEN.

HANSEN   [*looking at* MARGRJET] Why MARGRJET, ELSA could be my daughter; she has got my name.

MARGRJET   [*her face turning very red*] I wish she were your daughter, but I just had her christened HANSEN.

In the meantime, ELSA *has gone out of the room, and so to drop the subject,* MARGRJET *uses the opportunity to ask the Landlady to bring* ELSA *into the room to have her milk and cake, for very shortly she would have to go to bed, as it is already getting late.*

Coming into the room, little ELSA *looks a picture of health and beauty, with her fair long curly hair and big blue eyes. Every one of the people present has brought her a little present, which now they hand to her. She is so excited that she has no time to either drink her milk or even to eat the piece of cake she has so much looked forward to.*

The party is jolly, and, they are indeed all enjoying themselves extremely well, so one of the men, HANSEN it is, offers to bring his gramophone and records downstairs, so that they could have music. They play most of the records and as soon as little ELSA has gone upstairs with the Landlady, who has very kindly offered to let ELSA sleep with her, they start to dance. It is late, so the party has to finish, as everybody present has to get up in the morning. The men offer to see the other two girls home, and so it happens that HANSEN is the one who does not go. He puts his records in the covers again, but he cannot find the tin of needles he brought downstairs as well. So, they come to the conclusion that one of the two men must have put it in his pocket. So, HANSEN decides that he would stay up and wait for them to return.

MARGRJET   It was really very kind of you OSWALD to bring the gramophone down. It certainly made a lot of difference, so I am very thankful to you.

HANSEN   Not at all MARGRJET. I have enjoyed myself very much, thanks to you, and by the way you dance very well. Let us dance again, will you? [*He selects a record, a waltz it is. They dance and both thoroughly enjoy it. As it was very late* HANSEN *decides that he would leave the gramophone till the following evening. He thanks* MARGRJET *for the very pleasant evening and leaves.*]

This is the beginning of their very great friendship, and within the year they are married.

TWO YEARS LATER

For the first two years, they live in Reykjavik, then MARGRJET's *mother at Isafjord becomes very ill, so* MARGRJET *returns to her family home to nurse her, and takes* ELSA *with her.* MRS. JONSSON *dies after only few weeks.* OSWALD HANSEN *comes to Isafjord for the funeral.*

While he is there, he is offered a job, which he accepts, as MARGRJET *prefers to live at Isafjord, especially now then she has the house, which she has been born and brought up in.*

Few months later, as they were having their Sunday meal, HANSEN *suggests that they should all go and have their photograph taken.* When little ELSA *hears this, she becomes quite excited, and wants to have it done right away; so, they decide to do so. The photographs are very good, so* MARGRJET *sends some to her friends in Reykjavik. And as she still has one left, she decides to send it to* ALFRED *and to tell him about her daughter, her marriage and her mother's death.*

ALFRED *happens to be home when the letter arrives. He is quite surprised, for he has long ago given up hope that* MARGRJET *would write to him, and what really surprises him most is that* MARGRJET *has married a man named* HANSEN. *What a funny coincident! After studying the photograph for a while, he hands it to* MARIE.

MARIE   Oh, what a lovely photograph, and is not the little girl like her father. Don't you think so ALFRED?

ALFRED   [*looking very thoughtful*] Oh, what was this you said MARIE?

MARIE   I was just saying, that I think the little girl looks like her father.

ALFRED   I don't know. I think she is more like her mother.

MARIE   Perhaps she is like them both.

ALFRED   [*irritated*] Maybe, you are right, I am not good at seeing these things.

MARIE   I think it awfully kind of MARGRJET to write to you and send you this lovely photograph.

ALFRED   Yes, she is a very kind sort, and I am really glad that she is happily married. I think I will write her a few lines, just now to congratulate her.

MARIE   That is right ALFRED, and remember me very kindly to her, will you.

MARGRJET *receives a very charming letter from* ALFRED, *wherein he tells her, that he has not told his wife about* ELSA *yet, but that he intends to do so, or either tell his eldest son* KNUD *about her, when he gets a suitable opportunity. She shows the letter to her husband, and they discuss the matter, and what they cannot decide on is, whether to tell* ELSA *who her father really is, or leave it till she gets older. At last, they make up their minds to leave it till she would be able to understand it better.*

11 YEARS LATER

It is autumn, and great excitement in ALFRED's *house in Bolungarvik, for* EMIL *is leaving to go to a Commercial School, in Edinburgh, as he wants to become a business man and not a sailor.* EMIL *is now nearly 18 years old, and is to be away for about three years. He leaves by the mail-boat for Isafjord, where he is going to take a boat in a few days' time for Leith via Reykjavik.*

He stays at the Salvation Army Hostel at Isafjord.

The S.S. GULLFOSS *arrives on time at Isafjord, and is only stopping for about 18 hours. So, in the evening there is to be a dance held ashore, and* EMIL *is certainly not going to miss this dance. He goes onboard to see the ship, as he has not been on board a big ship before. As he is standing on the deck and looking round, a boy about his own age, in a white jacket and carrying a tray with some food, passes. Suddenly he looks back and asks* EMIL, *whether he was looking for somebody.*

EMIL	No, I am going with this boat to Leith, so I am just having a look round.
THE MESS BOY	That is alright, go ahead, and if you like I will show you the engine room.
EMIL	Thanks, that is great, can I just wait here for you?
THE MESS BOY	Yes do, I won't be long.

When they were down in the engine room, EMIL *asks* THE MESS BOY *whether he was going to the dance.*

THE MESS BOY	Rather, and I am taking a girl with me. Are you going?
EMIL	Well, I want to go, but I don't know anybody, so I am wondering whether I could go with you, but seeing you are going with a girl, it is different.
THE MESS BOY	But why not come with us, I am sure ELSA won't mind.
EMIL	Thank you so much, if you think it will be alright, I would like to come.
THE MESS BOY	You come onboard about half past eight, and if you cannot see me, ask for ARNI SIGURDSSON, that is my name.
EMIL	And my name is EMIL ALFREDSSON from Bolungarvik. Well, good-bye and I will see you again about half past eight.
ARNI	Bye-bye Emil.

EMIL *is just in time onboard again, for* ARNI *is ready, so they both go to* ELSA's *home. She lives in a very neat little house, not far from the harbour.* ARNI *knocks at the door, and a very nice-looking girl comes to the door. She has evidently only expected to see* ARNI *for she seems to get a little startled when she sees the stranger.*

ARNI	Hello ELSA, may I introduce you to a new friend of mine, EMIL ALFREDSSON from Bolungarvik. He is going with us to Leith. So, he wants to come to the dance tonight, and I knew you would not mind if I brought him along.
ELSA	Not at all. very pleased to meet you. Come right in both of you and take a seat. I will be with you in a minute again.

EMIL   Thank you.

ARNI   ELSA don't be long now, it is already 9 o'clock you know.

The band is already playing when they arrive. When ELSA *comes back from the cloak-room,* ARNI *and she dance right away, but* EMIL *goes to the corner where most of the young gentlemen are standing.*

ELSA   Where did you meet EMIL?

ARNI   He just happened to be looking round the boat, so I offered to show him the engine room. Then he asked if I was going to the dance, and I told him so, and further that I was taking a lovely girl with me. He did not want to come along with us, but I assured him you would not mind. So, we came along. Do you mind?

ELSA   Not at all, I think he is a most charming boy.

After the dance, they go to get a table, when they have done so, ELSA *sits down, but* ARNI *goes to get* EMIL. *As they have just reached the table* EMIL *asks* ELSA *whether she would dance with him.*

ELSA   With pleasure!

As EMIL *is not used to dancing, they do not get on very well at first, but very quickly they are dancing together charmingly. They talk and laugh. In fact, so much so, that* ARNI *who is watching them from the table, is not at all too pleased. They both come laughing to the table.*

ARNI	Well ELSA, have you taught EMIL to dance?
ELSA	He is getting on well, but I think he can do with another lesson shortly.
EMIL	Thank you, I take it that I may ask you to dance with me again.
ARNI	If you are going to teach dancing, I am going to be your first pupil.
ELSA	Let us drop this, and what about some coffee, have you ordered any?
ARNI	Yes, I have ordered coffee.
ELSA	That is splendid.

EMIL *and* ELSA *dance most of the evening together, and both thoroughly enjoy themselves. After the dance, both* ARNI *and* EMIL *take* ELSA *home.* ELSA *thanks them both for a very enjoyable evening; and says that she would come down to the boat to see them off in the morning. They say good-night with a handshake; then the two boys leave and are alone.*

ARNI	Well, what do you think of Elsa?
EMIL	I think she is an extremely nice girl. You are very lucky to be her friend.
ARNI	It looks to me that you and she are quite as good friends, if not better.
EMIL	Nonsense, we have only just met.
ARNI	But sometimes it does not take a long time to establish a firm friendship, or shall I say fall in love.
EMIL	Don't be silly ARNI.
ARNI	I am not blaming you for liking ELSA, because there is something about her which people cannot help liking.

EMIL   Well, here is where I leave you, so good night and thank you very much for taking me with you to the dance.

ARNI   Good-night, see you tomorrow.

The morning is indeed lovely, except for a little cold breeze it could have been a summer's morning.

EMIL   [*going down to the boat, carrying a suitcase in one hand, suddenly hearing a voice, which he seems to recognise. He looks back, and sees* ELSA *coming running after him.* EMIL *stops and lifts his cap.*] Good morning. Elsa, how are you?

ELSA   I feel fine, how do you feel after last night?

EMIL   I feel grand, and I had a very nice dream, all about you.

ELSA   No, isn't that strange? I was dreaming of you too.

EMIL   What did you dream, tell me.

ELSA   Really? I cannot remember what it was, but I do remember that it was all about you.

EMIL   I am going to tell you what I remember of my dream; let us go in here and have a cup of coffee, before going down to the boat. We have almost an hour.

ELSA   Thank you, I am so excited to hear your dream.

When EMIL *has ordered the coffee, he starts telling* ELSA *his dream.*

EMIL	I dreamt I was dancing with you, and when saying good-night, what do you think I did?
ELSA	I cannot guess, what did you do?
EMIL	I kissed you.
ELSA	You did, and did not you feel ashamed of yourself?
EMIL	No, I was thoroughly happy and pleased with myself; the only thing I regret is that it was only a dream. If it had only been real, I should still be feeling very happy. ELSA, as I am leaving and will be away for so long, I must tell you how much I like you, so I hope you will write to me occasionally.
ELSA	I will write to you with pleasure. If only you write to me first, and although we have only known each other for less than a day, I must tell you that I have enjoyed your company very much indeed. So, don't you forget to write to me.
EMIL	You can be sure I won't, and what is more I will try and study very hard, so that I need not be away longer than two and a half to three years in the most. For I am sure that even that time will seem a whole century to me, for I know I will be thinking about you all the time.
ELSA	Well, I am afraid we will have to be moving. It is only about 20 minutes till the boat leaves.
EMIL	Will you do something for me?
ELSA	Certainly, if I can. What is it EMIL?
EMIL	To give me a kiss.

ELSA	If it is really your wish EMIL, I will gladly do it.
EMIL	That's kind of you, and do not forget that you have got to remember that kiss for a very long time.

As no one is in the little coffee-room. They kiss.

EMIL	EMIL [*taking his arms away from* ELSA] If only I could stay here a little longer.
ELSA	No, EMIL, it will do you good to see a foreign country and to meet different people.
EMIL	It is too late now anyway to change my mind about going. So let us go onboard now.

They go straight onboard and to EMIL's *cabin, for they do not want to meet* ARNI *till they have had their farewell kiss.*

EMIL shuts the cabin door, and they are alone from the world. They kiss again, and EMIL tells ELSA that he is in love with her.

ELSA	I love you too Emil. [*she kisses him again*] Now EMIL dear, I am afraid I will be stranded onboard, if I do not go right now.

They hurry up on deck. ARNI *is standing just near the gangway; they go straight to him, and* ELSA *taps him lightly on his shoulder.*

ELSA	Hello ARNI.

ARNI	[*turning swiftly round and looks quite surprised to see them both*] Why, I have been looking for you, when did you come onboard?
ELSA	Only few minutes ago.
EMIL	How are you, ARNI?
ARNI	Hello EMIL, how are you?
EMIL	Fine, thanks.

The ship's whistle has gone for the third time, so ELSA *after bidding them both good-bye with a handshake, hurries down the gangway.*

She stands on the pier waving her hand to them till the boat has left, then she goes home.

EMIL *has a very good journey to Leith, and the family he is going to stay with are there to meet him. He is very happy, although, he does not go much out during his stay in Edinburgh. He writes letters to his family and to* ELSA, *and* ELSA *never fails to write to him by every boat.*

LIFE BACK IN ICELAND

ALFRED EIRIKSSON *is getting on well with his boats; he has two now.* KNUD, *his oldest son, is the skipper on the other.* MARIE *and* ANNA *are busy in the new house* ALFRED *has bought.*

MARGRJET *and* HANSEN *are very happy. However, they also know* ELSA *is writing letters to a boy named* EMIL EIRIKSSON *from Bolungarvik, so* MARGRJET *is quite worried, as she knows one of* ALFRED's *sons is called* EMIL. *So, she tells her husband that she suspects* ELSA *is in love with her half-brother.*

MARGRJET   This is all my fault for not having told ELSA long ago, who her real father was. This is really terrible OSWALD. For me to tell her now, I am sure it will break her heart. I don't know what to do, can you suggest anything?

HANSEN   I am afraid there is not much that can be done, except telling her the truth. And as you say it will break her heart. I think we should leave it just now, and try to find out from ELSA, something more about EMIL, or else if she would agree to going away, say for instance to Reykjavik, she might meet somebody there that she could fall for, and then the matter would straighten itself out.

MARGRJET   Oh, you are wonderful, OSWALD, that is an excellent idea. I hope she will agree to going away. Then I will write to my old Landlady and ask her to take care of ELSA.

HANSEN   However, I think we should not say anything until tonight to her, when we can sort of talk about our stay in Reykjavik, and how nice a time we used to have there.

They all three sit down to their evening meal, and are listening to the news from Reykjavik on the Radio, when MARGRJET *looks towards* HANSEN.

MARGRJET   You know, OSWALD, that sometimes I really miss Reykjavik and wish that I was living there.

HANSEN   I do not blame you; I feel that way myself sometimes.

ELSA   Why don't you move to Reykjavik? I think I would rather like it.

MARGRJET   You think you would like it, ELSA?

ELSA   Certainly, I would like it. You don't expect me to stay here all my life, do you?

HANSEN   Would you like to go to Reykjavik for a little holiday ELSA?

MARGRJET   That is a good idea. It would be a nice change for you, and I think it would do you a lot of good.

ELSA   What is all this, do you really mean that you would let me go to Reykjavik?

HANSEN   We might consider it, if you really want to go.

ELSA *stands up and goes to* HANSEN, *puts her arms round his neck and kisses him, then she also goes to her mother and kisses her.*

HANSEN *stands up from the table and goes over to his desk. He takes out a sailing list; he looks through it.*

HANSEN	MARGRJET, the GODAFOSS is leaving in four days, do you think ELSA could be ready to go then?
MARGRJET	Four days, yes, she could be ready. You phone up our old Landlady and ask, if she can put ELSA up. If not, I ask her if she can find a room for her, and tell her to let us know as soon as she can.
HANSEN	I am afraid we will miss her, especially as this is the first time she has been away from us, but this is the only thing that might save the situation without breaking ELSA's heart. Of course, I am not saying it will, but there is a possibility. The only other thing is to tell her the truth before it is too late.
MARGRJET	I know, but what can we do?

The GODAFOSS *arrives, and* ELSA *gets a letter from* EMIL, *saying that he would come home in about seven or eight months' time, as he is getting on well with his studies and in five months' time going in for the final examinations, which he hoped to pass.*

ELSA *is very excited over this news, and also over going away the following day.*

MARGRJET *comes in, just as* ELSA *has finished reading her letter, with a suitcase in her hand, which she has just bought for* ELSA.

MARGRJET	[*putting down the suitcase*]. From whom is the letter, ELSA dear?
ELSA	From EMIL; he is coming home in seven or eight months' time.
MARGRJET	What is he going to do then?
ELSA	I do not know. I expect he will try to find a job somewhere.
MARGRJET	I bought you this suitcase, do you think it will be large enough?
ELSA	Thank you, mother, it is lovely, just the right size.

HANSEN, MARGRJET *and three* GIRL FRIENDS *see* ELSA *off the next day.* ELSA *is in a very good mood. They all go down to her cabin. And when the time is almost up, they go on deck again and* ELSA *kisses them all good-bye.*

MARGRJET	[*with tears in her eyes*]. Now ELSA darling, you take good care of yourself and remember to write often.
ELSA	Yes Mother, I will write by every boat, and will I take care of myself.
HANSEN	Phone us up after you get there, and tell us how seasick you were.
GIRLFRIEND No. 1	ELSA, don't you fall for one of these big wrestlers in Reykjavik.
GIRLFRIEND No. 2	We will never allow you to get married so far away from us, so don't you try it.

HANSEN *and* MARGRJET *look at each other and nod.*

| GIRLFRIEND No. 3 | Never mind ELSA, they just envy you going away, and having a chance of meeting all these big shots in Reykjavik. |
| ELSA | Don't you worry, I will come back alright. |

They wave their hands, and the boat sails slowly out of the Isafjord harbour.

REYKJAVIK

ELSA *is very happy in Reykjavik; she receives her letters from* EMIL *regularly, and she writes to him by every mail. She comes down to breakfast a little earlier than usual this morning, so the Landlady, seeing* ELSA *sitting there reading the morning paper, starts a conversation.*

LANDLADY	I think I know the reason why you are so early up this morning ELSA dear, you are waiting for the postman, isn't that right?
ELSA	You are right, I certainly am, and what is more, I might get some news about when my friend is coming home, that is to say if I got any letter.
LANDLADY	Oh, I see, so your young man is coming home, that will be nice for you ELSA. Does he live in Reykjavik?
ELSA	No, but he might get a job here, if he is lucky.
LANDLADY	Yes, if he is lucky, or if he has some friends or relatives that can help him. It seems to me that everybody gets a job through somebody nowadays, and not because they are able or suited for the job.
ELSA	I don't think he knows anybody at all here, so from what you say, it will be difficult for him to get a job. But I know he is clever, therefore, I think he will get on alright.
LANDLADY	I am glad you have faith in him, there is nothing like trusting people, you know. Well, I have better go and get you some breakfast now.
ELSA	Thank you, I am feeling quite hungry now.

ELSA *has just started her breakfast, when the postman knocks and brings some letters for the Landlady, and one letter for* ELSA. *She knows the writing on it, so she goes up to her room to read it.*

Amongst other things EMIL *tells her about, is that he will be coming home in about three or four weeks' time, and that he has great hope of getting a job in Reykjavik in one of the banks.* ELSA *is so pleased to hear this, that she feels like jumping up in the air. So, she decides to sit down and write to her mother right away und tell her the good news.*

Two days later as ELSA *is just coming in for lunch, the telephone rings. The Landlady goes to the phone and is holding up the phone to* ELSA.

LANDLADY	ELSA, this is a long distance call for you. it must be your father, I think.
ELSA	[*coming to the phone*]. Thank you, hello, who is there?
HANSEN	Hallo ELSA dear, how are you? It is nice to hear your voice.
ELSA	I am fine, thank you, how are you and Mother?
HANSEN	Quite well, we are just missing you a lot, so we thought might be you would like to come home.
ELSA	But Father, I told mother in my letter that EMIL was coming home in three or four weeks' time, so naturally, I want to stay here, at least until he comes.

HANSEN	I know dear, but your Mother is feeling a bit lonely you know being all by herself in the house during the day, so we thought if you came home it would cheer her up a bit.
ELSA	Of course, I will come home Father, but could not I stay for about six weeks or so yet?
HANSEN	Well ELSA darling, the time is up, so I will talk it over with your Mother, and then phone you up again, so bye-bye just now.
ELSA	Alright Father, give my love to Mother, bye-bye.

EDINBURGH

EMIL *has now finished in the school, but cannot get a boat till after eight days, so he is just taking things easy. This is a Saturday afternoon, and the people he is staying with are going away over the week-end, and for the first time EMIL feels homesick, and wishes that he were back in Bolungarvik. He has been so busy studying that he has not had time to feel lonely, so he goes downstairs to talk to* MRS. HAMPTON. MRS. HAMPTON is pleased to see him and tells him that her sister, MRS. BURTON has invited him for tea the following day.

EMIL	MRS. HAMPTON, I think I will accept your sister's kind invitation for tea tomorrow.
MRS. HAMPTON	That is the idea, EMIL. They will be delighted to have you and I think that young BURTON will be home from school. So, you two should have lot in common to talk about; I am sure you will enjoy yourself.
EMIL	Thank you, MRS. HAMPTON, it is very kind of your sister to have invited me.
MRS. HAMPTON	Not at all, EMIL, they will enjoy having you, and hearing all about Iceland. I am phoning my sister a little later, so I will tell her that you are coming tomorrow.
EMIL	Thank you, MRS. HAMPTON.

EMIL *goes over to* MRS. BURTON's *house about three o'clock in the afternoon, and as* MRS. HAMPTON *has said, he finds* BURTON JUNIOR *there. He is full of life and very interesting. So,* EMIL *is enjoying himself thoroughly. When* MRS. BURTON *comes into the room and tells them that tea is ready, they all move into the next room.*

They are all jolly at the table, and the BURTONS *are asking* EMIL *question after question about Iceland.*

MRS. BURTON	Tell me, EMIL. What is it really like in Iceland? I have always imagined it as a snow-covered country, probably it is the name that gives one this idea. Isn't it awfully cold there?
EMIL	Well, to tell you the truth, I have found it much colder here, maybe, because the cold is damper here. We get real frost up there in the winter time, otherwise the climate there is really excellent and very healthy. It never gets very hot there in the summer time, for there is always a breeze from the sea, and as for other things, I think, we are really quite as fashionable as other nations, if not more so in fact.
MR. BURTON	Well, I must say that is very interesting, and I have a good mind to go there for a holiday someday.
BURTON JUNIOR	Yes, Dad, let us go next summer.

MRS. BURTON	You know we have arranged for our holidays this summer, so don't you think it rather early to start planning next years' holidays now?
MR. BURTON	There is no harm in thinking about it.
EMIL	If you do come, I hope you will come to the West Coast, at least if I am there at the time. Otherwise, if I should be in Reykjavik, I could always meet you, and show you round.
MRS. BURTON	Thanks EMIL, we will be sure to let you know beforehand, if we go.

EMIL *who is usually a little shy at first, feels quite at home with the* BURTONS, *for they were such charming people.*

After they have finished their tea. MRS. BURTON *asks them to move into the other room, so they all rise from the table, and* EMIL *shakes hands with* MR. *and* MRS. BURTON *and thanks them for the lovely tea (This is a custom in Iceland, to shake hands with the hostess and thank her for the food, as people stand up from the table.)*

MRS. BURTON	I am sorry you have to leave so early, EMIL, but I do hope you will come again before you go back home to Iceland.
MR. BURTON	Yes, do come along before you leave for your country, I will go and get your coat.

EMIL *is quite at a loss to understand why* MR. *and* MRS. BURTON *are talking about him leaving so early, for he is enjoying himself and does not want to go. But when* MR. BURTON *brings in his coat and helps him to put it on, he does not know what he has done that would make them think he wants to go home. However, he feels the best thing for him is to leave. So, he thanks them again, and goes to his home.*

The HAMPTONS, *when coming home in the evening, stop at* MRS. BURTON's *house to take* EMIL *home and are quite surprised to find that he has gone.*

MR. BURTON	Probably the tea upset him, for as soon as we rose from the table, he shook hands with us. So, I did not want to press him to stay longer, so we told him we were sorry he had to go so early.
MRS. HAMPTON	Why, that is just their custom in Iceland. When they stand up from a meal, they always shake hands with the hostess to thank for the food. Poor EMIL, he must have felt a fool.
MRS. BURTON	I should think we were the fools, please apologise to EMIL from us, and explain that we thought he wanted to go home, for we should have been delighted to have him longer.
MRS. HAMPTON	I am sure he will just laugh, when he knows what it is all about, for he has a very good sense of humour. Well, bye-bye, I will phone you tomorrow.

MR. and MRS. BURTON	Don't forget to explain our mistake to EMIL, bye-bye.

When they come home EMIL *is reading the Sunday paper. They tell him what has happened, and he cannot help laughing heartily, for this is a joke, indeed.*

At the breakfast table next morning, they are all laughing over EMIL's *handshake the previous day, when the doorbell rings,* MRS. HAMPTON *goes to see who it is.*

MRS. HAMPTON	A telegram for you, EMIL, please. [*handing the telegram to* EMIL]
EMIL	For me? Thank you. [*opens the telegram*] It is from my mother. She says that Father is seriously ill, and that I will have to come home directly, and not stop in Reykjavik. Poor Father, I am sorry, I wish I could get a boat right away, but I guess I will have to wait these five or six days, and then I will always have to wait again two or three days at Reykjavik for the boat to go to Bolungarvik. So, I hope I will have better news by the time I get to Reykjavik, for otherwise I might lose the chance of getting this job.
MRS. HAMPTON	I am sorry, I hope your father will soon be better again.
MR. HAMPTON	So do I, Emil.
EMIL	Thank you, it is most kind of you both.

EMIL *is very anxious to get home. He knows his father has a very weak heart and that is what he is afraid of might be the trouble with him now. The telegram from his mother has not mentioned from what complaint his dad is suffering.*

THE RETURN HOME

EMIL *is greatly excited when he wakes up onboard the* BRUARSFOSS *for now they have reached the Westman Islands, and they are only stopping there for few hours, and from there to Reykjavik it takes only about ten hours. But a sudden change comes over his face when the thought of his father's illness comes to his mind, but then again, he remembers that* ELSA *would be down at the pier to welcome him and, then again, his face gleams with youthful happiness.*

They arrive in Reykjavik at 9 p.m. Saturday night and there is a great crowd on the pier. EMIL *stands on the deck anxiously looking onto the pier; all of a sudden, his eyes rest on a girl, who is also looking anxiously for someone onboard. Then their eyes meet.*

Then ELSA is among the first visitors to get onboard and EMIL comes running forward to greet her. He puts his arms round her and kisses her.

ELSA   How very glad I am to see you again EMIL, and what a lot you have changed.

EMIL   And I can't tell you how pleased I am to see you again, and you look more beautiful than ever ELSA. But ELSA dear, I have got bad news. I can't stay in Reykjavik as I had planned, I must go home by the same boat; I got a telegram from mother saying father was very ill.

ELSA	I am sorry to hear that. I hope he is better by now, so that you can stay here. Otherwise, it is very probable that I shall have to go on this boat to Isafjord, for father phoned me the other day and told me that mother is feeling a bit lonely being by herself in the house all day, so if you are not going to stay here, I don't mind going at all.
EMIL	That is splendid ELSA; it gives us a little more time to talk about all the things we have seen and heard since we saw each other last, and now you must begin by telling me all about yourself.
ELSA	I am afraid it is not much I can tell you about myself. You will have to tell me all you know about Scotland, and all the wonderful things you have seen there like trains, buses and trams and what it feels like to travel in them. I am like a country girl and have only seen them in the films you know.
EMIL	Well, shall we go now. I am leaving my things here for I am sleeping onboard. Will you wait here a minute, I am taking my raincoat with me, better be on the safe side. [*back with his raincoat on his arm, and taking* ELSA's *arm*] Let us hurry, I shall be glad to put my foot on firm ground again.
ELSA	I quite believe that, but where are we going?

EMIL	I was hoping you would invite me to your room; you don't live so far away, do you?
ELSA	No, it is not far away, but I cannot even offer you a cup of coffee there, so I think we should go to the Hotel Esja first and have a cup of coffee and listen to the music.
EMIL	That will do fine.

They reach the Hotel Esja, which is as crowded as usual, especially on Saturday nights. ELSA knows quite a lot of the people there, and everybody turns round to see who her new friend is. As they sit down the waiter came, they order two cups of coffee and some cakes.

EMIL	[*after looking round*] Have you been here often ELSA?
ELSA	Not very often, but there is not much we can do here, except go to the cinema or come for a cup of coffee here, and as the cinema is more expensive, I prefer to come here and listen to the lovely music.
EMIL	But you can't come here by yourself, can you?
ELSA	No, of course not, I go with my girlfriends; you don't think there is anything wrong in coming here, do you?
EMIL	No, but it seems so strange to me. And now ELSA dear, let me tell you something more important.
ELSA	That is better, tell me something about yourself.

EMIL	Will you marry me? I don't mean right away, but when I have really got a job.
ELSA	Do you really mean this?
EMIL	Of course, I am serious, you know I love you more than anything else in the world ELSA.
ELSA	You know I love you also with all my heart, so certainly I will marry you.
EMIL	But I want to ask you another question.
ELSA	What is that EMIL dear?
EMIL	Are you absolutely sure that you love me, and that you will be quite happy to settle down with me?
ELSA	Anything else you want to know?
EMIL	So, it is really true that you will marry me?
ELSA	Of course, I mean it, you know I do.
EMIL	I am the happiest man in the world. Let us dance this dance; it will remind us of the first dance we went to together, when we first met.

The band is playing the Blue Danube, and they dance it, as if there is not anybody else on the floor, although it is absolutely packed. So that there is really no need to dance; you could just move with the crowd. It is half past eleven, the big lights are put out, a sign that it is closing time. The band stops playing, EMIL *and* ELSA *go to their table, finish their coffee, then go out.*

EMIL *suggests that they should take a little walk. So, they walk out of the town a bit, where they can sit down all by themselves. They talk about the happy days they would have together when they will be married etc. etc.*

ELSA	Well EMIL darling, I have made up my mind. I am going home on the BRUARFOSS, so that we can have a little more time together, and even if we are not in the same place, I feel that I am nearer to you, if I am at home than if I was here!
EMIL	That is splendid ELSA; I am glad you are going back home. I know you are in good hands there, and as you say we will be nearer each other than if you were in Reykjavik. [*gets up suddenly*] ELSA, my darling. It is getting very late, so what about getting back shortly.
ELSA	It is so beautiful out here. I could stay here all night.
EMIL	[*puts his arms around* ELSA *and they kiss*] Yes, it is lovely here, but I was thinking of getting up reasonably early. I want to try and see the bank manager about the job in the bank, that I had every hope of getting. I also want to tell him the reason for my having to go to Isafjord and home instead of waiting here till I was to start on the job. That is to say, if I get the job. So shall we go now?
ELSA	Right you are, let us go then.

EMIL *goes to the bank the following morning, and has to wait a long time before he can see the manager.*

THE MANAGER	[*opening the door*] Who is next?
EMIL	[*rises from his seat*] Good morning, Sir.

THE MANAGER	Good morning. Oh yes, you have come about the job I mentioned I might be able to find for you.
EMIL	Yes, Sir.
THE MANAGER	I am afraid there is nothing for you just yet, but probably in a month's time or so; at least I will do my best to help you.
EMIL	As a matter of fact, that will suit me even better for I have to go home first, as I have had a telegram from my mother, saying that my father is very ill.
THE MANAGER	[*rising from his chair*] In that case I will write to you and let you know.
EMIL	Thank you very much Sir, good-bye.
THE MANAGER	Good-bye.

EMIL *goes to see* ELSA *right away to tell her the news.* ELSA *is just getting ready to go out, when* EMIL *arrives.*

EMIL	Hallo darling, how are you this morning?
ELSA	Fine thanks. Did you see the manager?
EMIL	Yes, I have seen him, and he has no job for me at the moment, but probably after a month or so.
ELSA	That is splendid, congratulations. [*walks towards* EMIL *and kisses him*]
EMIL	Thank you darling, I am so happy.
ELSA	So am I, dear.

ISAFJORD

When the boat lands at Isafjord, MR. *and* MRS. HANSEN *and some of* ELSA's *friends are on the pier to meet her.*

EMIL *is standing by* ELSA's *side and she is pointing her father and mother out to him. As soon as* MR. *and* MRS. HANSEN *are onboard,* ELSA *rushes forward with* EMIL *following her, to introduce* EMIL *to them, and to her girlfriends. After kissing* ELSA, MR. *and* MRS. HANSEN *try to greet* EMIL *as cordially as they possibly could, although,* MARGRJET *cannot help, not feeling quite at ease.*

They all go to ELSA's *home, where chocolate and coffee is awaiting them, not forgetting all the cream cakes etc.*

EMIL	[*as soon as they have finished their coffee,* EMIL *rises from the table*] You will have to excuse me, I should have liked to stay longer, but I will have to find out when the next boat leaves for Bolungarvik.
MARGRJET	Yes, ELSA told us about your father's illness. I am sorry EMIL; I hope he will soon be better.
EMIL	Thank you, MRS. HANSEN. [*turning to* ELSA] Good-bye just now, but I will be back as soon as I have been able to find out when the next boat leaves.
ELSA	Alright EMIL, I will stay here till you come back, bye-bye.

It so happens that there is a boat leaving in less than half an hour's time, and EMIL *decides to take it, as otherwise he would have to wait overnight. So, he has just time to rush back to* ELSA's *house to take his belongings and say good-bye.*

EMIL
Well ELSA, darling, I will have to leave right away, there is a boat going in few minutes' time. So don't forget to write, and I will be back as soon as my father is well, or at least as soon as I hear something further about the job. [*He shakes hands with* MR. *and* MRS. HANSEN, *but* ELSA *goes to the hall with him, where they kiss good-bye.*]

BOLUNGARVIK

The little boat arrives two hours later at Bolungarvik, KNUD *and* ANNA *are down at the pier to meet* EMIL.

EMIL   Hallo KNUD [*kisses him*] Hallo ANNA [*kisses her*] and now tell me how is Father?

KNUD   Hallo EMIL, I am glad you are back. Father is still very ill, but we hope for the best.

EMIL   I am sorry to hear that, and how is Mother? I expect she has been busy and therefore not able to meet me.

KNUD   She is fairly well, yes, she has had a busy time. You know what Father is like when he is not well, and this of course is the worst illness he has ever had.

ANNA   You have changed a lot EMIL, and what about this girlfriend you wrote me about?

EMIL   You have changed a lot too ANNA, you are quite an old lady now. Well to tell you about my girlfriend, she is at Isafjord just now, she was on the same boat as I from Reykjavik.

ANNA   Oh, you need not tell me anymore then.

EMIL   You don't want to hear any more? I am surprised. Well, here we are, even the house has changed. This one looks much better than the old one did, at least from the outside.

MARIE [*opens the door and runs towards* EMIL, *swings her arms around him and kisses him*] What a big man you are EMIL, welcome home. It is good to see you again, after all this time.

EMIL Oh Mother dear, how lovely. It is to see you again, and to be home with you all, only I wish Father had been well.

MARIE Yes EMIL dear, if only your Father was well [*wiping tears from her eyes*], but we hope for the best.

They go into the kitchen, where MARIE *has been busy baking pancakes etc. for* EMIL.

EMIL [*noticing the cakes*] Mother dear, you should not have taken all this trouble to bake for me, when you are so busy and tired [*goes to her and kisses her on the forehead*]

MARIE EMIL, it is a pleasure to bake a few of your favourite cakes, and now come in to greet your Father, and then the chocolate will be ready.

They go upstairs to ALFRED's *bedroom. When they come in,* ALFRED *lifts his head from the pillow slightly.*

ALFRED Hello EMIL, it is good to see you again.

EMIL EMIL How are you FATHER? It is fine to see you again [*bends down and kisses him*].

MARIE   I think we should go down and have the chocolate now, then afterwards you can come upstairs again and have a little chat with your, Father.

EMIL   Yes mother. See you again in few minutes Father. [*They leave the room.*]

They all sit down in the dining-room to have their chocolate and cakes, which they seem to enjoy very much, although no one says very much at the table. Just when they are about to finish there is a knock at the door.

MARIE   Come in.

Two boys enter. They are old friends of EMIL *and the family.*

FRIEND   We were just too late to meet you when
No. 1   the boat came in EMIL, so we had to come and see you.

FRIEND   Tell me EMIL what is it like in Scotland, did
No. 2   they give you plenty to eat?

EMIL   Hello boys, nice of you to come. Hey, do I look as if I have not eaten anything, since I left here? Well to answer your question, I can tell you the people were both extremely kind and most generous in every way, so I certainly cannot complain.

MARIE   Come in and sit down, boys. Have a cup of chocolate with us.

FRIEND   Thanks very much, I can never say no to a
No. 1   cup of chocolate.

FRIEND   No, you could not, neither can I, so thanks
No. 2   very much.

KNUD *stands up to get more chairs; then the boys sit down, but* MARIE *goes to the kitchen to get more cups, chocolate etc.*

The boys talk quite freely at the table, but MARIE *and* ANNA *are rather quiet; they are more concerned about* ALFRED's *illness.*

When they have finished KNUD *goes to his father's bedroom just to see if he is asleep; he opens the door very quietly and peeps in.*

ALFRED	[*seeing the door opening*] Who is there?
KNUD	It is me, Father. I was just seeing if you were asleep.
ALFRED	When you boys have finished your coffee, I want to have a talk with you, so tell EMIL to come in when he has finished will you.
KNUD	Certainly, Father. [*closes the door quietly and goes back to the dining room*] EMIL, Father wants to have a talk with you or rather us when you have finished your chocolate.
EMIL	Yes KNUD, I am just finishing.
THE TWO FRIENDS	[*having also finished their chocolate, rise and thank for the chocolate*] Well EMIL, it is nice to have you back home again, so we will be seeing you. So bye-bye for now. [*They leave the house.*]
KNUD	EMIL, if you don't mind, I think we should see Father right away, so that, when we are finished, he can have a sleep.

EMIL   Very well, we will go right now. I wonder
              what is on Father's mind.
KNUD   He is just worried about Mother and us,
              and wants to talk about the future to us.

They stop outside the bedroom door, and KNUD *opens it very carefully.*

ALFRED   Come in boys, I have something I want to
              tell.

They come in, move two chairs nearer the bed and sit down.

EMIL   [*whilst sitting down*] Father I have got
              something to tell you too. It is about ELSA,
              the girl I wrote Mother about. We are
              going to get married as soon as I have got
              a fairly good job.
ALFRED   I was afraid of that. It is in connection with
              that I want to speak to you.
EMIL   But Father, she is a very nice girl, so why
              say you were afraid of that?
ALFRED   I am sorry EMIL, but I have to tell you the
              truth, although, I know you will both be
              very disappointed, especially you EMIL
              my boy [*strikes his forehead and eyes and
              continues in a lower voice*] ELSA is my
              daughter. [*then he breaks down and cries*]
              I hope you will forgive me, although, I
              should have told you sooner, and please
              don't let your Mother know this, for it
              would break her heart.

EMIL   [*excitedly*] But surely Father, this cannot be right, are you sure you are talking about the same girl.

KNUD   Come now EMIL, Father is quite exhausted. (*putting his hand on his Father's shoulder*) You have a rest now, Father. We will not mention this to Mother or any other person; you can be quite sure of that.

ALFRED   EMIL, my son, can you forgive me? And try to do the right thing for both of you. For you cannot marry her, not that you know the truth.

EMIL   [*bends over his Father and kisses him*] I have forgiven you Father, and I will try to find a way out somehow, so don't you worry anymore Father.

ALFRED   ALFRED. I am proud of you son. You have taken this like a man would do. [*pats EMIL's shoulder*]

KNUD *and* EMIL *go out of the room together. They hesitate a second outside the door.*

KNUD   I am sorry EMIL. This is very sad, but please for Mother's sake try to be as cheerful as usual so that she won't guess that something is up.

EMIL   Thank you, KNUD. I will do my best. I was just thinking about ELSA. It will be very hard for her.

KNUD	Here comes Mother, we will just tell her that Father was saying, that he hoped that we would carry on with the boats, and take care of her and ANNA.
MARIE	How is your Father?
KNUD	Just the same Mother, only a little tired.
MARIE	What did he want to see you about?
EMIL	He was just saying, that he hoped we would carry on with the boats and so on.
MARIE	I will just go in and see if there is anything he wants.
KNUD	No Mother, he is alright. He just wants to have a rest, so don't disturb him.
MARIE	Very well, KNUD, I will just go and wash the dishes with ANNA. You boys will have plenty to talk about.

EMIL *and* KNUD *both go down to the sitting-room.*

KNUD	[*as they are sitting down*] What about writing to ELSA and telling her the truth?
EMIL	I cannot do that, although, I know her mother would tell her that I was telling the truth. I dread to think what might happen to her. But I know she is full of pride, so if I broke our engagement, I know she would just go and marry someone else, and show me that I was not the only man in the world. No, just give me time to think, I cannot realise all this yet.

The next morning MARIE *gets up first as usual. She goes into* ALFRED's *bedroom.*

MARIE [*opening the door*] Good morning, ALFRED dear, I hope you have had a good sleep.

But no answer comes. So she goes to the bed; his eyes are wide open, she feels his hands. They are cold. Then she knows the worst has come. He has died. She buries her head in her hands, sits down on the bed and cries. A few minutes later she stands up again, and goes into the boys' bedroom. She goes to KNUD's *bed and shakes him lightly. He opens his eyes.*

KNUD Mother, what has happened you look so pale?

MARIE Not so loud KNUD. I want EMIL to sleep longer. He will be tired after his journey.

KNUD But what is it, Mother?

MARIE It is your father, come with me.

KNUD [*gets up at once and puts his dressing gown on*] Is he worse mother?

By this time MARIE *is out of the room, and* KNUD *follows her to his Father's bedroom. And as soon as he sees his Father's eyes open, he knows that he has gone. So, he walks towards the bed and draws the sheet over his Father's head. Then he takes his Mother's arm.*

KNUD   I know this is terribly hard for you Mother and for us too, but don't worry Mother, we will all be alright. [*They walk quietly out of the room and go downstairs.*]

A few minutes later, ANNA *and* EMIL *come downstairs, and they quickly see that something has happened. So,* KNUD *tells them very gently that their Father is dead. They all sit down in the sitting-room, except* ANNA *who goes to the kitchen to get their breakfast ready.*

Immediately after breakfast, EMIL *sits down to write a letter to* ELSA. *He tries to write in the usual way, but finds it very difficult. He tells her about his Father's death, and in fact very little else.*

ELSA *receives the letter two days later, and she thinks there is something strange about the way* EMIL *has written, but she put it down to, that the reason would be his Father's death. So, she does not give it much thought. She tells her mother about* ALFRED's *death.*

ELSA   I think I will write EMIL just now to tell him how sorry I am.

After EMIL *has received* ELSA's *letter he decides that rather than let* ELSA *think that he has changed his mind about her, he would take a trip to Isafjord, and talk to* ELSA's *mother first, and get her to help him to tell* ELSA *the truth. Then they could part like friends, he knows it would be equally hard for them both, but he is determined that this would be the best.*

THREE WEEKS LATER

It is about three weeks now from his father's death, and everything seems to be taking its usual shape again, except that EMIL *seems to be more alone and not so cheerful as he used to be, but his friends think that he is worried over his father's death. But* KNUD, *who knows the real reason, tries to do everything he can to make things easier for* EMIL.

The mail-boat is leaving the next morning for Isafjord. So, EMIL *tells his mother that he is thinking of going to Isafjord for a few days.*

The boat arrives at Isafjord about noon and EMIL *goes straight to* ELSA'*s home. He knocks on the door, and none but* ELSA *herself comes to the door and opens it.*

ELSA	Why EMIL, this is a surprise. [*puts both hands round his neck and kisses him*]
EMIL	Yes, I know it is a surprise, but I had to come and see you it is very important. Is your mother in?
ELSA	Yes, she is in, you sound very strange. What is wrong? Tell me. Aren't you pleased to see me again?
EMIL	Certainly, ELSA, you know that, but I should like to speak to your mother for few minutes alone, if I can.
ELSA	Of course, but come in and have some coffee with me, I am just having a cup myself. Then you can speak to mother afterwards. You are not in any hurry, are you?

| EMIL | No, but I would just like to see your mother first. If you don't mind. |
| ELSA | If you insist, just go to the kitchen. She is there, she will be glad to see you EMIL. I will be in the sitting-room. |

MARGRJET *is preparing lunch, and as soon as she sees* EMIL, *she knows what is up.*

MARGRJET	[*drying her hands*] Hello EMIL, I did not expect to see you here, however, I am glad to see you.
EMIL	I expect it is a surprise [*they shake hands*] and how are you MRS. HANSEN?
MARGRJET	Quite well, thank you. I was sorry to hear about your father.
EMIL	Thank you. MRS. HANSEN. Could you spare me a few minutes, I should like to talk to you, before MR. HANSEN comes home for lunch.
MARGRJET	Certainly EMIL. I think I know what you want to tell me, I am indeed very sorry.
EMIL	My father told me about ELSA being his daughter, just before he died. And you see what makes it so hard is that ELSA and I love each other, and we were going to get married as soon as I had got a good job.

MARGRJET	[*patting* EMIL *on the shoulder*]. I know my boy. It is really all my fault, I should have told ELSA long ago, and I can tell you it has not been easy neither for me nor my husband, since we knew ELSA had met you, and was writing to you. But we were always hoping that something might happen that would separate you two, without having to break your hearts by telling you the truth. However, I am glad your father told you himself before he died, and that you came to me. Have you thought what you are going to do EMIL?
EMIL	How do you think it will be best to tell ELSA?
MARGRJET	I think we should both go in right now and tell her the truth, I know ELSA is a sensible girl, so I hope she will be as brave as you.
EMIL	I think that will be the best.

They go together into the sitting-room. ELSA *is standing at the window. She turns round as they enters the room and walks towards them.*

ELSA	Well, here you are then, and what have you been doing, plotting something against me, or what is all this about?

MARGRJET	ELSA dear, there is something that I should have told you long ago, but I had not the courage, but now I have got to tell you.
EMIL	It is about me ELSA or rather us. You will have to be strong and face the truth, it has not been easy for me, but I have taken this course to come and tell you myself with the help of your mother.
ELSA	I don't understand all this, what are you trying to tell me? For goodness' sake, come out with it, then I will know what it is all about.
MARGRJET	You are EMIL's half-sister.
ELSA	What EMIL's half-sister? This is impossible [*looks to* EMIL *then her mother*]
EMIL	I know how you feel ELSA dear, for I feel the same way myself, but it is the bitter truth, and we will have to face it.
ELSA	[*sits down on the sofa and buries her face in her hands. Then she starts shouting.*] Why had this to happen to us, why has this been kept from me so long?
MARGRJET	ELSA, I hope you will forgive me, it is a terrible thing but I know you are both such very sensible young people.
ELSA	Sensible, that is good, when one's future is all smashed up, for no fault of our own.

EMIL	It is no use trying to put the blame on anyone, my father told me this, the evening before he died, and of course it was the greatest shock of my life.
ELSA	I know EMIL dear, I am sorry. [*drying her eyes and standing up*] Well Mother, Father will be here any minute, so I will set the table. [*as she is walking towards the door to leave the room, she turns round*] By the way Mother, does Father know about this?
MARGRJET	Yes, he does, ELSA dear.
ELSA	I just wondered.
EMIL	Well, I will go now and get a room at the Salvation Army Hostel, but I will come again and see you before I go back home again.
ELSA	What nonsense! We have got a spare-room here, and you are certainly not leaving before you have had lunch with us.
EMIL	Thank you I will have lunch with you, but I would rather take a room at the Hostel. Thanks all the same for offering me the room.

After lunch EMIL *goes to the Salvation Army Hostel and gets a room. Then he walks down to the harbour, where he hears that the S.S.* GULLFOSS *is expected to arrive the following morning.*

| EMIL | [*talking quietly to himself*] That is excellent. I will go onboard and see ARNI, and I will take him to ELSA's house. He will cheer her up, I am sure. |

The GULLFOSS *arrives about 11 o'clock the next morning, and* EMIL *is onboard shortly afterwards. He stops to ask a deckhand. who is working on the deck, where he could find* ARNI. *The man tells him where* ARNI's *room is, and* EMIL *goes there. Just as* EMIL *comes to the door,* ARNI *opens it and comes out, ready to go ashore.*

ARNI	Now, what is this! Am I dreaming or is it my old friend EMIL? Why this is a surprise, I did not expect to see you here.
EMIL	And what is this I see, am I talking to the Captain of the ship or what? Hallo ARNI, it is nice to see you again, how are you?
ARNI	I am fine thanks, and sorry but you are only talking to the Steward, and what is worse, ELSA is still thinking about you, and does not look at me, not even now that I wear a uniform, so there you are. I expect you are here to see ELSA?

EMIL	Yes, I am here to see ELSA, but, on the other hand, I am also looking for a job, for I am not so sure that I want the job in the bank. I think the sea might suit me better after all. You see my father died the other day, so my brother KNUD and I will have to support the home. Talking of ELSA again, she might look at you yet ARNI, so don't you worry.
ARNI	I don't think I have got a chance against you EMIL, however, I am not worrying. I am sorry to hear about your father, but I think you are right about the job, the sea is better for you.
EMIL	Come on ARNI, let us go and visit ELSA. And this is no joke, I wish I could get a job as a deckhand or something, that would do me nicely to start with.
ARNI	Do you mean that?
EMIL	Of course, I mean it.
ARNI	I have got an idea, there is a deckhand needed onboard, but the Captain was going to leave it till we got back to Reykjavik, but if you are ready to take the job, I will speak to the Old Man.
EMIL	I have not got all my clothes here, but I could send mother a wire right away. Which port do you call at next?

ARNI	We are stopping here about 24 hours, then we go to Flateyri, and we are stopping there about two days, for there we take fish and fishmeal. So, you should have ample time to get your clothes, if you get them sent on to Flateyri.
EMIL	In that case, if I get the job, mother can send my trunk to Flateyri.
ARNI	Let us go and see, if the Captain has gone ashore yet.

ARNI *and* EMIL *both go to the Captain's Cabin.* ARNI *knocks on the door.*

CAPTAIN SIGURGEIRSSON	[*sitting at his desk*] Come in.
ARNI	[*opens the door*] I am very sorry to trouble you, Captain, but I would like to speak to you a minute, if I may.
CAPTAIN SIGURGEIRSSON	No trouble at all. Come in.
ARNI	And I wish you to meet a friend of mine EMIL ALFREDSSON, CAPTAIN SIGURGEIRSSON.
CAPTAIN SIGURGEIRSSON	Pleased to meet you, and where do you come from young man?
ARNI	I come from Bolungarvik.
CAPTAIN SIGURGEIRSSON	From Bolungarvik. Oh, I am also from Bolungarvik. That is to say we used to live there once. What did you say your name was?
EMIL	EMIL ALFREDSSON.

CAPTAIN SIGURGEIRSSON	Not by any chance a son of ALFRED EIRIKSSON?
EMIL	Yes, I am his son, but I am sorry to say I lost my father only a few weeks ago.
CAPTAIN SIGURGEIRSSON	I am very sorry to hear that. I used to know him well many years ago, and I have always remembered him since.
ARNI	What I really came about CAPTAIN, was to see if EMIL could get a job as a deckhand?
EMIL	I should be very grateful CAPTAIN, if you could possibly help me.
CAPTAIN SIGURGEIRSSON	Alright, my boy, we will sign you on tonight, when we can talk further about the job, duty, salary and so on. By the way, I expect you know the salary is only 220.- Krona per month?
EMIL	Thank you, CAPTAIN, I will try to do my best.
CAPTAIN SIGURGEIRSSON	Don't mention it, come again about five o'clock, I shall be onboard then.
ARNI and EMIL	Good morning, CAPTAIN, and thank you very much.
CAPTAIN SIGURGEIRSSON	Good morning, to you both.
EMIL	[after having left the cabin] Thanks, ARNI, that is great. I will send mother a wire right away. Then we can go and see ELSA.
ARNI	I will go with you to the Post Office first, then we can go together to ELSA's house.

When they have sent the telegram, they walk to ELSA's *house, and* EMIL *knocks on the door this* time. It is MARGRJET, *who answers the door. She shakes hands with them both and asks them to come in. And she tells them that* ELSA *would be down in a minute.*

MARGRJET	Did you have a good trip, ARNI?
ARNI	Yes, very good indeed; the weather was fine all the way.
MARGRJET	I am glad to hear that, although, I expect that you men are all such good sailors, that you don't mind what the weather is like.
ARNI	We get used to it.
EMIL	Well, I am going to try the sea.
ARNI	He has just got a job with us you know.
MARGRJET	Really, as a cook?
EMIL	No, as a deckhand.
MARGRJET	And do you think you will like that EMIL?
EMIL	I think so, MRS. HANSEN. I don't think an office is really the place for me.
MARGRJET	Perhaps, you are right, EMIL. I expect you have got the liking for the sea in your blood. [MARGRJET *leaves the room.*]
ELSA	[*enters the room*] Hello EMIL, hello ARNI. (*walks to* ARNI *and shakes hands with him*] Did you have a good journey?
ARNI	We could not have had better weather all the way.

EMIL	Hello ELSA, how are you? I hope we are not disturbing you, coming unexpected like that.
ELSA	Not at all, I am very pleased to see you both.
MARGRJET	[enters the room in overcoat and hat] I am sorry; I have got to go out, but ELSA, you make some coffee, and there are some cakes in the pantry.
ELSA	Yes, mother I will make some coffee shortly, bye-bye.
MARGRJET	Bye-bye. [leaves the room]
ELSA	You put on the radio, boys, and I will go and put the kettle on.
ARNI	Why not let us all go out to the Cafe instead?
EMIL	That is a good idea. Come on ELSA.
ELSA	Thanks very much, but it is no trouble to make a cup of coffee here.
ARNI	Come on, ELSA, we are just in time for the afternoon dance.
EMIL	That will be like old days again, you remember when we all three went to the dance?

They all go to the Cafe, and as they enter everybody looks up, and ELSA nods her head to several of the people. Then they sit down, and just as they do so, the girl who plays the piano starts to play, and her first tune is the waltz EMIL and ELSA had danced after, the first time they met. They look at each other. ARNI remembers the waltz very well too, so he is quick to notice how they look at each other. Then suddenly EMIL gets up.

EMIL	ELSA, will you dance this dance with me?
ELSA	[*looks up at EMIL*] With pleasure.
ARNI	Perhaps you will be good enough to dance one dance with an old friend later?
ELSA	Certainly ARNI.
EMIL	[*whilst dancing*]. You know ELSA, ARNI is still as fond of you as he was, and he is really a very nice person.
ELSA	I have always been very fond of him, but not the same way as I felt about you, but don't let us talk about anything sad. I want to remember this last time we are together with pleasure and not with sadness.
EMIL	But ELSA this is not our last time together; surely, we can see each other, although it will be different to our former friendship.
ELSA	Of course, we will see each other again, and I will never think of you with other than pleasant memories, and as a charming and honest man and friend, and I hope we will always be friends, and as you know you are always welcome to our house.

EMIL   We will always be friends ELSA, and
                thank you for all your kindness, but in
                the future, I am afraid my home will be
                ships and the sea. But there is one
                thing I will always have with me and
                that is the memory of you, which I will
                value more than anything else in the
                world!

The dance is over, and they go to their table and sit down.

*After a short interval, the girl starts playing again. This
time,* ARNI *and* ELSA *dance together,* and *somehow or
other from this moment a much deeper affection and
friendship begins between them, and within eight months
they are married.* EMIL *acts as* ARNI's *best-man. They are
very happy, and* EMIL *is their true friend at all times.*

SEVEN YEARS LATER

EMIL *is now the* CAPTAIN *of the* S.S. GULLFOSS, *with* ARNI *as his* STEWARD, *and they are still the best of friends.*

This is New Year's Eve, the GULLFOSS is on its way to Reykjavik from Copenhagen. The CAPTAIN and other Officers, as well as the Crew, are all sitting in the ship's dining-room. Some of the men have, although it is only about half-past nine, already have had a little too much to drink.

EMIL	[*rises from his chair and walks to* ARNI] What about sending ELSA a telegram, ARNI; she will receive it tomorrow morning, if we send it now.
ARNI	Oh yes, I had nearly forgotten. She will be delighted to have a telegram from us. I will go down and write it out just now. [*stands up and leaves the room*]
EMIL	The Wireless Operator is up in his room; just take it to him. He will send it right away, and don't forget to send my good wishes as well. [*Then* EMIL *also walks out of the room.*]
A MEMBER OF THE CREW	[*just after* EMIL *has left the room*] I wonder why such a very handsome and kind man as the CAPTAIN should not have got married long ago.
ANOTHER MEMBER OF THE CREW	That is very simple. He was once engaged to ARNI's wife, then she let him down to marry ARNI, and I think he is still in love with her.

FIRST MEMBER OF THE CREW	Nonsense, do you think that he would be so friendly with ARNI and his wife, if she had let him down. Anyway, he can still get married. So don't you worry!
SECOND MEMBER OF THE CREW	Well, I still think that he is in love with ARNI's wife, and that he will never get married.
AN OLD GENTLEMAN	[stands up and leans over the table] Well, if you want to know the truth: it was said that the CAPTAIN's father was also the father of ARNI's wife, so now you see why they did not get married.

Just as he has said this, the door opens and ARNI comes into the room, and the men change their talk quickly over to other things.

THE END

GUÐBJÖRG ELINBORG ÞÓRÐARDÓTTIR

Born: 8 August 1908, Isafjord, Iceland
Died: 4 July 1983, London, England

Gudbjorg Elinborg Thordardottir was born on the 14th of August 1908 in Isafjordur, Iceland, daughter of Fridrikka Engilbertsdottir and Thordur Bjarnason. Fridrikka came from Dyrafjordur in the Northwest Fjords and had moved to Isafjord to work in the fishing industry. There she formed a relationship with Thordur, a

Isafjord, 1908

fisherman from Akranes and Elinborg was born. Thordur was already married and had a family in Akranes and would only be in Isafjord during the fishing season.

As Fridrikka was a single mother, she had to earn a living by working in the fishing industry, which was the predominant industry in Isafjord but was seasonal. To fill the gaps, she took cleaning jobs, but times were hard and money was short.

Frederikka, 1935

At school in Isafjordur, Elinborg made friends with Maeja Helgadottir, daughter of the local Bank Manager. Maeja was to remain her very good friend for the rest of her life, and the kindness and generosity of her family were a great help to Elinborg, providing her with clothing, second-hand and new, for special occasions which Fridrikka could not afford.

Elinborg and Maeja,
1920, Isafjord

Iceland, 1930

After finishing school, Elinborg and Fridrikka moved to Reykjavik and Elinborg took on a job at VerzluninEdinborg, the best-known retail store in Reykjavik, owned by Asgeir Sigurdsson, who was also the British Consul and his office acted as the British Consulate in Reykjavik. While working in the store, Elinborg joined the Verslunarfelagid Merkur, the trade association for shop and commercial workers and after three years became head of the women's section, which she was to remain until leaving Iceland. She started working in the office and was sent to the Pitman's School in

Manchester to learn shorthand and speed-typing in English, having studied English the previous winter.

While working in the Consulate side of the office, Elinborg was able to help visiting sailors and businessmen with their language problems by acting as a translator. At that time, the first freezing plant in Iceland, the Saensk-Islensk Frystihus, was being built and equipped and a number of British engineers were involved in the construction and fitting out of the plant and installation of the machinery. Through her translating work, Elinborg came to meet her future husband, James McDonald Ferrier, who was overseeing the installation work.

James McDonald, 1920

They became engaged and were married on the 16th of July 1932, with the reception at the house of Asgeir Sigurdsson. They moved to England and settled in Forest Hill, Southeast London.

James was a departmental manager for a large fish importing company, Bennetts of Billingsgate, involved in the buying of overseas fish. Their first child, Edda Elinborg was born in

James McDonald, 1930

October 1933, followed by a son, James Arthur, in December 1934.

In 1937, Elinborg took the children to Iceland and visited her friends and relations in Isafjord and Reykjavik. Her mother, Fridrikka, returned with them to London, and was to remain with them in Forest Hill until she died on the 5th of May 1943, surviving the Blitz in wartime London. In 1937 also, they moved to a larger house in Forest Hill, perched on a hilltop, with a splendid view over London. This house was to become a favoured destination for many visiting Icelanders.

When war broke out in 1939 and the bombing of London began, the blitz as it was known, the children, Edda and James, were evacuated to Devon first, then Manchester staying with the people that Elinborg had stayed with during her Pitman's study course, and then Liverpool.

The bombing seemed to follow them around and in 1942 it was decided to bring the children back to London. At the start of the war, Elinborg and her husband joined the ARP, the Air Raid Protection squad, which patrolled neighbourhoods at night to help in case of fire and damage from enemy bombing. They both served until the end of the war.

In October 1943, their third child, Frederick Charles was born. During the war, through her contacts with the Icelandic Embassy, Elinborg was asked by the BBC Overseas Service to do information broadcasts to Iceland, which she was very happy to do. She was also a founding member of the Icelandic Society in London, which was formed to provide a network for Icelandic girls who had married British servicemen and come to live in England, and also for Icelandic businessmen and doctors who were resident in England. Elinborg later became President of the Icelandic Society, an honour she greatly appreciated.

At the end of the war, Elinborg established her own Export/Import and Manufacturers Agent business, G.E.Ferrier Ltd, first working from home and then moving to offices in Westminster.

Business was mainly exporting goods to Iceland, Norway, Denmark and Sweden and Iceland constituted the bulk of the business, although there was a notable success in supplying Italian clothing to the Magasin du Nord in Copenhagen in 1948. The business was very successful until the 'Cod War' between Britain and Iceland began and Iceland banned the import of British goods.

Elinborg then turned to retailing, which she had learned at

Verzlunin Edinborg, and bought a retail business in Greenwich, South East London, a Drapery, selling ladies hosiery, underwear, corsetry, children's clothes, haberdashery, dress fabrics and specialising in knitting wools. The export/import business was relocated above the shop. A few years later, Elinborg purchased another shop in Orpington, Kent, Lloyds and it was there that she was to spend the rest of her working life, retiring in 1980.

Elinborg was a keen member of the Orpington Chamber of Commerce and was Chairman for a period and then Vice President. Lloyds moved to larger premises in Orpington in 1972 and the Greenwich shop was sold in 1974, replaced by a Fabric Shop in Tunbridge Wells, in Kent, which was run by her son Frederick. In the Orpington shop, Elinborg was able to enjoy the company of three fellow countrywomen, who had come to London after the war as wives of British Servicemen, Hulda Whitmore, Dua Mountain, and Betty Lilley, whose company and work were much appreciated.

Following the death of her husband, James McDonald, in 1965, Elinborg had sold her house in Forest Hill and had purchased one in Orpington, more convenient for work. On retirement in 1980, following the sale of Lloyds, Elinborg moved in with her son, James Arthur, and daughter-in-law Gudrun Jonsdottir, at their house in Chelsfield Kent, and was able to enjoy three years of retirement before her untimely death, due to a heart-attack in July 1983. One of her proudest moments was the award of the Order of the Falcon for services to the Icelandic Society in London over many years, the award being presented by the Icelandic Ambassador in London on the 12th of February 1970.

SPEED CERTIFICATE

This is to Certify that

ELLA THORDAR

has been examined by the undersigned
Examiners, and has satisfactorily passed a test
in Pitman's Shorthand at the rate of

EIGHTY

words a minute

Alfred Pitman
Ernest Pitman

Phonetic Institute
Bath

14 JUNE 1928.

A Full Certificate for Theoretical and Practical knowledge of Pitman's Shorthand is granted when a Theory Certificate and a Speed Certificate or Instructor's Certificate for not less than eighty words a minute have been obtained.

Taught by *Amy C. Edwards*

Metropolitan Borough of Lewisham.

TOWN HALL,
CATFORD, S.E.6.

his is to Certify *that*

MRS. G.M. FERRIER

of 67 Lipbook Crescent, S.E.23.

has completed a Course of Anti-Gas Training held under the auspices of the Council of the Metropolitan Borough of Lewisham and has acquired sufficient knowledge of Anti-Gas Measures TO ACT AS

AN AIR RAID WARDEN

Nature of Course attended FULL COURSE

A.A. LIID, A.R.P.S.

Name and profession of Examiner.

John T. Duff

Town Clerk.

Date 15th October, 1940.

The conditions governing the award of this certificate are shown overleaf.
This certificate is to be regarded as of local validity only.

Printed in Great Britain
by Amazon

32386140R00066